SHOT ON LOCATION

Shot On Location

A Key West Mystery

Laurence Shames

The characters and events portrayed in this book are fictitious. Any similarity to real persons, living or dead, is coincidental and not intended by the author.

ISBN-13: 978-1491241455

For Marilyn

And for everyone who does the work and doesn't get the credit

PART 1

1

When the call came in, Jake Benson, ghostwriter extraordinaire, was pinching dead leaves from the last remaining basil plant on a windowsill of his Upper West Side apartment.

It was January in New York and a good old-fashioned cold snap was killing everything that was not already dead. The houseplants, starved of daylight, alternately chilled by drafts and baked by the dry heat of the radiators, had no chance. Often the curling, desiccated leaves didn't even need pinching; they could be made to fall off just by looking at them. Jake didn't know why he bothered with houseplants. No, actually, he did know: They gave him something to fiddle with when, as now and for the past few months, he was between gigs. When he wasn't writing, he didn't quite know what to do with himself. More than that, he wasn't quite sure, even at the age of forty-two, who he was. Was he a guy who liked fiddling with houseplants? Who sometimes thought about getting a cat? Moving to France? Taking up the saxophone?

His tendency was to audition these various versions of himself until his next paid work came in, at which point he put aside the diversions and the fantasies and took refuge in the one thing the world had told him he was good at: writing other people's books. For this he had an almost freakish knack. He could write on any subject, from diabetes to race car driving to World War I; assume the tone of any genre–self-help, romance, confessional memoir; mimic any voice, whether that of an aw-shucks athlete, a business bigshot, or a messianic fraud. He had no idea how he did this, but it came to him so easily, called for so little real involvement, that it had been years since he'd seriously wondered if he actually enjoyed it. It was how he made his living. It was what he did.

Now, one hand full of brittle leaves, he picked up the ringing phone. And sure enough, the call was from his agent, Lou Mermelstein.

"Jake," he said after the bare minimum of chitchat, "great news! Just heard about a terrific gig for you. Something a little bit different. A tie-in novel with one of the hottest shows on television."

Benson had been waiting for a call like this since late last summer. That didn't mean the call made him happy, only that he'd been waiting for it. Now that the call had come, his first impulse, as ever, was to resist. "Lou, I don't write for television. You know I don't write for television."

"Who said this is writing for television? It's a book. A book that goes with the show."

"A book, yeah. One of those crappy paperback novelizations with the cheesy covers."

"Jake, are you listening? Not a novelization. A free-standing book. A tie-in."

"Tie in with what?"

A little sheepishly, Mermelstein said, "With…with the mythology of the show."

"Say again?"

"The mythology. Look, I don't know what the fuck it means either. It's how everybody talks in television."

"Exactly. Which is why I'm not interested."

Mermelstein squeezed the little tension-reducing squeezy-ball on his desk. He'd worked with Jake Benson for quite a few years, knew him pretty well. Like all writers, an odd duck, with a core ambivalence that just wouldn't quit. He wanted this gig. He *needed* this gig. The agent was sure of it. Still, it was typical that he'd start by saying no. It was his pattern. The details varied, but he did it every time. He railed, he mocked, he subverted. He just had to. He used wry and scathing negativity as a warm-up the way some people used calisthenics.

Soldiering on, the agent said, "Don't you even want to know the name of the show?"

The writer said nothing.

"*Adrift.*"

"Never heard of it."

"Strictest confidence? Until a week or two ago, I hadn't either. Which just proves that you and I are out of it. It's been on the air maybe five, six episodes and it's already top-ten in the ratings. People love it. The critics love it."

"Television has critics? Now there's a gratifying job."

Mermelstein let the comment pass. "So the show," he went on, "it's based on a tried and true formula, old as *Robinson Crusoe* or even *Gilligan's Island.* Survivors under palm trees."

"Oh for Christ's sake, a reality show?"

"Not a reality show. That's the genius part. It *looks* like a reality show. Smoking hot twenty-somethings in shredded clothing. But in fact it's a good old-fashioned serialized melodrama. Carefully scripted. Overlapping stories."

"Overlapping stories? You mean it's a soap opera."

Through the phone came an almost audible wince. "Don't call it that. Especially not if you talk to the producers. They'd be really offended."

"Good."

"So here's the set-up, all established in episode one. There's these people on a cruise ship. Not some dorky, Carnival Lines kind of cruise ship. One of those big fake sailboat cruise ships that young, hip, single people might be on. You with me so far?"

"I've never seen a hip person on a cruise ship."

Mermelstein ignored him. "So they're in the middle of the ocean—"

"Which ocean?"

"Who cares? An ocean's an ocean. So they're in the middle of the ocean, and there's a giant earthquake, and the earthquake raises an enormous tsunami, eighty, ninety, a hundred feet tall; and the tsunami catches the ship, and the ship rides it like a surfboard;

rides it thousands of miles at hundreds of miles an hour, rocketing along like it was on top of a twenty-story building. And after hours of incredible terror, the tsunami finally hits an uncharted reef in the middle of nowhere, and the ship is smashed to smithereens, and all the navigation stuff is destroyed, and all the less attractive people get drowned, except for like two old ones and one fat one to make it seem more like a slice of actual humanity, and they make it ashore where the better-looking people start having sex with each other and learn to survive against mysterious forces while waiting for however many seasons to get rescued, unless they never get res-cued because they're already dead but have no way of knowing it."

Jake Benson said, "And all this happens in episode one?"

"In like the first five minutes. It's set-up, backstory. Then it plays out from there. So whaddya think?"

"I think I'm gonna puke."

Purely for his own amusement, Benson actually stuck a finger partway down his throat. He was still rather playful, occasionally goofy, for his age. In part this came from working alone, doing his thing with no one watching; in part it came from a lifelong though lately atrophying tendency to play the entertainer. In this his looks conspired. He was in equal measure handsome and funny-looking—quite tall, very thin, with brown, curly hair that twirled the occasional ringlet over his ears or down onto his forehead, a rather eggish forehead that made his hazel eyes seem more than halfway down his face. The usual expression on his full lips was more complicated than a smile but gentler than a smirk and suggested a more or less constant musing on some private joke.

The agent said, "I knew you'd like it. But the tie-in part, what they want from you, it's a book, a novel, supposedly being written by one of the minor characters—"

"Whoa, whoa. Written by one of the characters?"

"Yeah," said the agent. "You know, a story within the story. A metafiction."

"Sounds gimmicky as hell."

"One man's gimmick is another man's bold postmodern master-piece. But will you let me finish? So this character, we never actually meet him, but he's like a savant, a psychic, and his novel somehow holds a lot of obscure but fascinating clues as to what's really going on in the show. So they refer to the book in a later episode. Then the book gets published–"

"In the show?"

"Not in the show. How could it be in the show? The show's on an island in the middle of nowhere. No, the book gets published in the real world, and fans of the show buy it with real money, and they look for clues and they talk about it online, and ratings go up and the producers and the network and even the poor bastard publisher, which is owned by the same giant conglomerate as the network, make even more money. It's, you know, it's synergy."

"I hate that word."

"Who doesn't? But it's what they call it."

"So wait a second. Let me make sure I have this. I'm supposed to write this fucking book, and then it comes out under the name of a minor, made-up character who never even puts in an appearance?"

"That's kind of the deal."

"And the book probably becomes a bestseller and as usual nobody ever knows I wrote it."

"Yeah, there is the usual gag clause."

Benson bit his lip, looked over at the dead plant on the window-sill. "How the fuck did I end up in this line of work?"

"How? Or why? I can offer several reasons. You like to eat. You don't see the inherent nobility of manual labor. You—"

"All right, all right."

"Come on, cheer up," said the agent. "They're offering one-fifty."

Not a princely payday in some professions, a hundred-fifty grand was a top-tier gig in the ghostwriting business. Mermelstein paused a moment to let the figure sink in.

"We might even get them to go two hundred. They're under crazy deadline pressure. They need a polished manuscript in ten weeks. There's like six people in the world who can do a decent book in ten weeks. They need a total pro, an ace, a first-rate, can't-miss, completely reliable craftsman."

Benson said, "I love it when you suck my dick. But who are the other five?"

"Let's not name names. There's no one better. Besides, the others probably aren't available."

"You've tried other clients?"

"Jake, will you stop? I haven't tried anybody else. You're my first choice. You're the editor's first choice, you're everybody's first choice. Absolutely."

"Now you're blowing smoke up my ass."

"Look," said Mermelstein, "I'm very good at what I do, but not even I can suck your dick and blow smoke up your ass at the same time. Pick one…Oh, and there's one other thing you should know about the show. It's shot in Key West."

"Excuse me?"

"Key West. The Keys. That's where they're shooting, on a tiny island just outside of town. You'd have to spend two or three weeks down there. Expenses paid, of course. It's eighty-two degrees there now. I just checked."

Benson, uncharacteristically, found himself at a loss for words. His subversion was suddenly thwarted, his complaints cut off at the knees. Over the course of a long silent moment he glanced once more at the dead plant on the sill, the trapezoids of frost behind it on the windowpanes, then felt an expansion, an opening outward, behind his eyeballs and at the top of his head. Key West! He'd always wanted to go there, had never quite got around to it. Now someone was offering to send him and pay for it; in January, no less. He pictured yellow sunshine, balmy evenings, mangoes. He imagined the coconut smell of suntan lotion on bare and glistening skin. "Key West?" he finally intoned. "Christ, Lou, why didn't you say that at the start?"

"I was saving it. In case I needed a clincher. The producers want you to spend some time around the set, picking up on, you know—"

"I know, I know. The mythology."

"Exactly. I knew you'd catch on. So you'll do it?"

"Get the bastards to go the extra fifty grand and I'm on it."

"I knew you'd say that. I already got you the extra fifty."

"You're a manipulative dick."

"Love you too. Don't forget the sunblock."

2

The next day, on the set of *Adrift*—on a mangrove islet that appeared to be in the middle of nowhere, though as the pelican flew it was a mere dozen miles from Southernmost Point—things weren't going all that well. The caterer, hung over, was late with lunch. A microphone boom had been bent double by a falling coconut. But the main trouble centered, as it often did, on Candace McBride.

Candace was one of the stars of the show and, while the cast was purportedly an ensemble, it never would have occurred to her to doubt that she was the main attraction. She was stunningly beautiful but what was compelling about her was the way she combined a few different and seemingly irreconcilable kinds of beauty. She had thick black hair and wide-set violet eyes that were movie-star glamorous by any standard. Yet her small and slightly snub nose was strictly girl-next-door. Her broad and mobile mouth said sex kitten, but her strong legs and rather square behind said Title IX. In the show, she played Lulu, the woman that all the men wanted. This was not a big leap from her role in real life, except that in real life people got to know her well enough to change their minds.

Now the cast was sitting in sling chairs in the shade of some palms, doing a read-through of that week's episode, which was about the survivors' efforts to come up with a plan for governing themselves and allotting their scant resources. The rehearsal was going smoothly enough until Candace said, "Wait a second, I can't say that line. I'll sound like a fucking idiot."

The producer looked at the director. The director looked at the line producer. They were trying to decide whose turn it was to deal with their diva. Finally, the director, Rob Stanton, said, "Okay, Candace, what's wrong with the line?"

"My whole backstory, my whole arc," the actress said. Her voice was as multifaceted as her beauty. Somehow it combined a breathy purr with the hard edge of habitual complaint. "My character's sharp, hip, with it. She's not gonna go around quoting Abe Lincoln."

"Abe Lincoln?" said Stanton.

The actress gave a contemptuous shake to the script in her hand and slapped at the offending passage. "*Oh,*" she read, "*so it's like all animals are created equal but some are more equal than others.* That's Abe Lincoln, right? I think it was in the movie. Gettysburg Address or some shit."

There was a silence. People looked down at their hands or up at the sunlight as it sliced through fronds. The producer, Quentin Dole, visiting the set from his usual perch in Los Angeles, tried to hold back a sigh.

"Actually," he said. "It's George Orwell." He paused and looked around the circle of blank faces. "That name ring a bell at all?"

A breeze blew and made a scratchy sound in the foliage. Finally an actor raised his hand as if he were in class. "*Brave New World,* right?"

"Close," said Dole, who was thirty-nine, had fashionably close-clipped hair, and wore those West Coast glasses with titanium frames and lenses that were always getting darker or lighter. He was one of the creators of the show as well as the head of its writing team, and he stood to make tens of millions of dollars from it. Now he summoned patience and said, "*Brave New World* was Aldous Huxley. Orwell wrote *1984*. And also *Animal Farm,* where this quote comes from."

"And which no one gives a flying crap about," said Candace.

"I completely disagree," said Dole. "True, most people won't catch the reference. But a few will. And that's part of the mythology—"

"Oh Christ," the actress interrupted, "not this mythology bullshit again. I'm just trying to learn my lines and get through the day."

"The mythology," the producer resumed, "that gets people talking and keeps them coming back. Say two percent of the audience gets the quote. They post, they tell their friends. Right away, it's hey, there's clues in Orwell, check him out. So the show expands outward—"

"Spare me, Quentin. You sound like a goddamn professor. Reminds me why I quit college. But I'm not saying that fucking line. Give it to someone else."

The star glared at the producer. The producer glared at the star. Then a woman spoke up softly. Her name was Claire Segal and her job title was line producer. What this meant, in effect, was that she was the person all sides bitched to. All problems—budgets, scheduling, nervous breakdowns–eventually became her problem. She was a cross between the school nurse and the Secretary of State. For this complex role she received decent but not fabulous pay and no glory whatsoever. In a soothing voice that played no favorites, she said, "I have an idea, kids. Why don't we take a little break and all calm down?"

3

Just then Jake Benson's puddle-jumper was landing in Key West. He'd left behind a fresh wet snow in New York, and, his tireless ambivalence aside, he had to admit he was feeling pretty good. Traveling on a gig and with a purpose. After vague and logy months of fiddling with houseplants and wondering if he would ever actually try the saxophone, he was once again alert, focused, engaged with the wider world as it trundled along its screwball course.

The dinky plane taxied to the dinky terminal, the propellers stopped, the door was opened. Jake moved to the top of the stairway, squinted toward the flame-white sky, and was immediately hit under the chin by the first warm blast of Key West air. The air was weighty, almost liquid, and it had a complicated and ancient smell. It smelled of salt and iodine and toasted seashells, and underneath these tangy aromas was a darker, low-tide whiff of slight decay, not fetid, not cloying, but carrying an oddly comforting suggestion of rot, of things calmly and slowly breaking down, of life returning to its original goo. The sunshine didn't seem to slice straight through this viscous air; it seemed somehow to mix with it, to stir it, to lift it in folds and curls like a spoon in batter. The breeze came in scraps, moments of hot stillness in between. By the time he reached the pavement, that very morning's slush seemed to belong to a different geologic era.

He walked toward the terminal, a small suitcase in one hand, his laptop slung over the opposite shoulder. Feeling jaunty, carefree, he was whistling. His arrangements had been made for him. A driver was supposed to meet him. This was one of the small but pleasant amenities of being on a job: The driver deferentially holding up a card with *Mr. Benson* written on it.

Except when the writer reached the terminal, there was no driver with a card.

There were drivers with cards for other passengers but not for him. He scanned the quickly thinning crowd and tried not to look like he'd been stood up.

Then, after a couple of long minutes he heard quick footsteps tapping sharply along the floor. He looked up to see someone rushing toward him—a wiry fellow, maybe just smaller than average, the tan face looking forty or so, but with a forward, avid lean to his gait that suggested someone younger. The man had thick black hair and wore rather large sunglasses with dark blue lenses. From a step or two away, he said, "Jeez, I'm sorry to keep you waiting. My greeter flaked out on me today. Conflict with an estrogen injection or something. Happens around here. It's the Keys. What can you do? Mr. Burton, right?"

"Benson."

"Benson. Sorry. With the television people, yes?"

Absurdly, the writer felt the need to make a fine distinction. "*With* them, no. Working *for* them. I do books."

"Ah. Books about TV?"

"Not exactly. Sometimes. It depends."

"Well, anyway, good to meet you." Extending a hand, the other man said, "Name's Goldman. Joey Goldman. Come on, I'll bring you to your place. Lemme have that bag."

At curbside, parked illegally, they found a white '70s vintage El Dorado convertible, lovingly waxed against the salt and the rust. The top was down, the hot red upholstery gleamed in the sun. "Nice ride," said Benson, climbing in. His irritation at being kept waiting had somehow evaporated in the sunshine. This was surprising. In New York, when he got annoyed, it lasted longer, sometimes years.

"Lemme tell ya something about this car, Mr. Benson—"

"Jake."

"Lemme tell ya something about this car, Jake. It's wider than the streets and burns gas like a fighter jet. But I'll never part with it. You know why? This is the car that brought me here. From Queens to the promised land, almost twenty years ago. You from New York too?"

"Born and bred," said Jake. Actually, he'd lived in New Jersey until going off to college, but why admit it if you didn't have to?

They'd turned out of the airport and were driving along the seafront now. There was a broad promenade between the ocean and the road. People zigged and zagged along it on a dozen different kinds of boards and skates and bicycles with whitewall tires. Women who shouldn't have been were jogging in bikinis. The water was green but not a see-through green; it was milky from the coral dust that mixed in from the bottom.

"First time down here?" Joey asked.

"Florida, no. The Keys, yeah."

"Two completely different places. Florida, that's golf and prunes. The Keys...they're not exactly peace and quiet. Maybe more like peace and mayhem."

"You wouldn't think those things would go together," Jake observed.

"Right. You wouldn't. Except that sometimes down here they do. And another strange thing. It's funny, what happens to New Yorkers down here."

"What happens, other than that they get a sunburn and act undignified?"

Joey laughed. "Well, those things for sure. And most people, they come down for a week, ten days, they go home, they peel, it's over. But the New Yorkers who really get the feel of the place..." He tailed off, pulled both hands from the steering wheel, and shrugged.

"What?" said Jake. "What happens to them?"

"I dunno," said Joey. "I'm not that good at explaining things. But this town gets to people. Things start looking different. What matters, what doesn't. What's allowed, what isn't. What's real, what's bullshit. People surprise themselves here. They change. You'll see.

Or maybe you won't, I dunno. I guess it's like catching a cold. Some people get it and some people don't. Who the hell knows why?"

In the baking metal shed that served as her on-set office, Claire Segal was sipping hot green tea as Quentin Dole poured himself a tonic water.

"I just don't see how you do it," the producer said.

"Hard to believe, but I enjoy young actors."

"No, I meant the tea. How can you drink hot tea when it's a hundred degrees in here?"

"A hot drink actually cools you off. Try it sometime. But about the actors, you know, they're growing up in public. Can't be easy. Look at the bright side, no one's totally snapped so far."

"Don't even say that kidding around."

"Who said I was kidding?" At that Claire flashed one of her characteristic expressions—a widening of the eyes coupled with a quick raise of the eyebrows and a small lift of the chin. Her eyes were a surprising light green. Her hair was reddish brown, now sharply highlighted by sunshine; on set, she wore it tightly pulled back, out of the way, almost invisible. That, and the fact that she was over thirty, prevented most people from noticing that Claire was actually more beautiful than many of the tall and skinny actresses around her. Her skin, even underneath a surface coat of suntan, had a peachy cast, a glow. She was fit and toned and yet she had some flesh on her--an actual woman of brains and sinews rather than a stretched and air-brushed fantasy of one.

Quentin put his tonic water down. It instantly sweated a wet ring onto the cheap plastic table. "So who's our leading candidate?"

"For snapping?"

"You think it's Candace?"

Claire didn't need long to think it over. "No, not Candace. She's a bitch but she won't flip out. She's got that knack of blaming everyone else for everything. So who else? A couple of the guys seem pretty fragile. But the one I worry more about is Donna."

The producer hesitated just slightly. "Donna? Who the hell is Donna?"

"Maybe you haven't even met her. She was hired out of Miami. The stunt girl, the body double. Donna Alvarez."

"Oh, right," said Quentin. "I guess I've seen her head-shot. Not so pretty in the face."

"Pretty enough for most things. But I agree, not a stunner. Her only flaw. Other than that, she's amazing. An uncanny match for Candace. The height, the figure. Plus she can really act, not that she gets a chance to. But she's wound very tight and she has an awful lot of time to sit around feeling left out. It's a concern. We'll see."

Quentin finished off the last of his drink. "Well, I head back to L.A. tomorrow. It's your zoo after that."

"While you get to work with that famously sane and reasonable group, the writers."

The producer blew some air between his lips. "Yeah, they're a handful, too. At least some of them know George Orwell from Abe Lincoln. Oh, and I meet this other writer for a drink tonight. The one who's doing the tie-in book."

"Right. Yeah. What's-his-name."

"What's-his-name," Quentin Dole echoed with a shake of his head. "There you have it. A-list ghostwriter, half a dozen bestsellers on his resume, and he's still a what's-his-name. Must be very shy. Or maybe just clueless about what it takes to make it big."

4

The El Dorado had turned inland and was lumbering through a quiet neighborhood. Jake blinked and considered an odd impression: Everything except the car he was riding in seemed suddenly miniature.

Tiny vehicles, scooters mostly, were parked at the curb. Tiny dogs patrolled miniscule front yards. Here and there, in front of tiny shops dispensing Cuban coffee, little men sat on low stools playing dominoes. The neat pastel houses were narrow and close together, their porches barely deep enough for dollhouse rocking chairs; even the palms that hung over the roofs seemed toylike. Sometimes two homes shared shade from a single tree, like lovers huddled under the same umbrella.

So this was Key West, Jake thought. Famous Key West. Legendary Key West. He'd expected it to be bigger. Without really thinking about it, he'd figured it had to be bigger to accommodate the folklore. But in fact the island was a mere speck, a broken off nodule of a ruined reef, a sandbox for kids pretending to be grownups or for grownups trying to steal a little of the goofy joy of being kids again.

Jake became aware of Joey's voice and realized that he hadn't been listening for a while. He said, "Sorry, what's that?"

Joey said, "I was saying that this place you're gonna be staying, I think you'll like it. I used to live there myself. First place I ever had down here." Joey smiled at the reminiscence. Even through the blue sunglasses Jake could see his eyes go soft and wider. "Came down as a short-term renter and a real putz. Now I own the place. The whole compound. God bless America."

Jake didn't exactly know what a Key West compound was, but it sounded substantial and he tried to look impressed.

As it turned out, the compound was a sort of postage-stamp Club Med. Inside a rustic fence made of plants that grew so close together that not even light came through, there was a pathway of white gravel leading to a small but beckoning free-form pool and a sunken hot tub ringed with an apron of blue tile. Shaded by spreading Poincianas and quivering palms, a cluster of cottages was arrayed around the common area. The cottages were exuberantly mismatched, a yellow one, a turquoise one, one that had a fake thatch roof with the real roof showing through. There was a communal gas grill and a rack of unlocked bicycles, the beach-cruiser kind.

Joey pointed over toward them. "Take one whenever you like. Best way to get around town."

Jake nodded, took it all in, and a simple, boyish exclamation escaped him. "Man, this is nice!"

Joey beamed, then looked down modestly as he led the way toward the yellow cottage. "Kind of a funny story how I got the place," he said. "The former owner, my landlord, was a nice guy, a little odd. Used to just stand naked in the pool all day."

"Naked?"

"Yeah. It's clothing optional. They didn't tell you that?"

"They didn't tell me anything."

"Well, anyway," Joey went on blithely, "few years ago this guy calls me up. 'Joey,' he says, 'I got big problems. The vacation market is in the shits, I can't pay my mortgage. What should I do?' I say, 'How about you put some fucking pants on and get a job?' He says, 'I have no pants.' I say, 'I'll buy you some.' 'No,' he says. 'Fuck pants. How about you buy the place?' So I bail him out, he disappears one day, and here we are."

Joey finished the story just as they reached the cottage door, and, with a bit of a flourish, he threw it open. Inside, there was a vacuum cleaner standing in the middle of the living room, its cord snaked across the floor, its plug connected to nothing. A young fellow in a faded red sarong was sleeping on the sofa, his cheek resting angelically on his hands.

"Oh Christ," said Joey. "Bryce!"

With no great urgency the man in the sarong bestirred himself and opened one eye. "Oh, hi Joey."

"Hi Joey my ass. Get up off the couch."

Bryce scratched his head. His feelings seemed hurt. "You don't have to yell at me. The place is clean. I just got sleepy."

To Jake, Joey said, "I'm really sorry. It usually isn't like this…No, let's not bullshit, it's like this a lot of the time. Look, I manage other houses. Plus we have hotels here. If you think you'd be happier…"

Jake was looking around the living room. It had louvered windows through which the rustling of palm fronds could be heard. The furniture was old rattan, scuffed and scarred in places, with faded floral upholstery. A lazily turning ceiling fan dangled overhead; its oversized blades spread a faintly narcotic aroma of jasmine.

"No," he said. "I'll take it. It's fine. Just what I would've pictured if I'd had time to picture anything."

Joey Goldman seemed not just relieved but genuinely pleased. "That's how I felt too. Saw the place, saw naked people, guys in skirts. My first thought: What the fuck? Then it was like something just let go and suddenly it all seemed fine. What a place down here should be. Well, here's my card. You need anything, just call. Come on, Bryce, grab the vacuum cleaner and let's let Mr. Benson settle in."

5

Jake put his suitcase on the bed and began looking for ways to make the place his own. The first priority, of course, was settling on where he would write; he chose a small desk in an alcove near a bedroom window. Then he propped his shaving kit behind the faucet of the bathroom sink. He checked out the kitchen and found a wineglass and a coffee cup that were good enough. It was while he was in the kitchen that he heard the altercation by the pool.

It was a terse and basic altercation. He heard the compound gate whoosh open and slam shut, then Bryce said to someone, "I really don't think you should be here." The tone was languid and mild but held a firm note of moral certainty.

The answer came back quick and nasty. "Mind your business, faggot."

There was a brief pause, then Bryce, still mild, unshaken, said, "You shouldn't go in there. She isn't home."

The other man, apparently of limited vocabulary, said, "I told you mind your business. I got a key. You don't think I got a key?"

There was the click of a door opening, then another pause, a slightly longer one, then the door clicked shut again. Bryce said, "Hey, you shouldn't take that. It isn't yours."

This time the answer didn't come in words. There was a momentary scuffle, so one-sided that it barely made a sound. Just a single low grunt and a quick small whimper. Then there was a splash.

Jake got to the window just in time to see Bryce righting himself in the pool, his sarong floating up around his legs like a dying tulip or a dirndl skirt. A large man in tight black shorts was leaving through the yanked open compound gate, kicking out a thick leg to clear the fabric from his butt crack. The gate slammed closed behind him, quaking on its hinges for a second or two, then all was quiet once again.

Peace and mayhem, Joey had said. Maybe there was something to it. Jake gave a private little shrug and went back to his unpacking.

A little while later, in the glorified shed back behind the pool pump and filter where he lived rent-free in exchange for chores, Bryce was sulking in his damp sarong. This wasn't because he'd been called names and tossed into the pool; that really didn't bother him at all. He was sulking because Joey was mad at him.

He felt he'd let Joey down and that this was fated to happen again and again because Joey didn't really understand him. Joey thought he was just a slacker. Which, admittedly, he was. But the part that Joey didn't quite get—what hardly anyone really got—was what his slacking was about. It's not that he was lazy. True, he spent an awful lot of time lying in his bed or on any convenient couch. But when he did so he wasn't just lying there; he was doing something else as well. He was waiting. Waiting for something worth getting out of bed or off the couch to do. This waiting wasn't passive; it was active and suspenseful. In fact it was exhausting, the more so because he had no idea what it was he was waiting for, or if it would ever come, or even if he'd recognize it soon enough if it appeared right there in front of him.

So he had to stay ready and he needed to be alert, if only drowsily alert, poised to identify his moment and to pounce on it. It was this dull but constant buzz of anticipation that was fatiguing, that made him need a nap after skimming half the pool or testing the pH in the hot tub or vacuuming the new guy's living room. That's the part he badly wished he could get Joey, or anyone, to understand. The waiting part. The staying ready. The numb suspense that gave a secret drama to his entirely uneventful life.

6

At twenty of six, showered and changed, Jake was ready to head to the Flagler House hotel for his meeting with the producer of *Adrift.*

He strolled past the now vacant pool and over the white gravel path toward the compound gate. He'd intended to walk to his appointment but then he saw the rack of bicycles. Best way to get around town, Joey had said. The only problem was that Jake hadn't ridden a bike in probably twenty years, except for stationary ones at the gym, and those did not tip over. But he did have his goofy side, and a sudden feeling of what-the-hell had overtaken him, and he grabbed a cruiser, a purple one.

He rolled it through the gate, mounted very gingerly, as if climbing onto a horse that might shy, and wobbled off. The seat was much too low for him and his bony knees cranked high and splayed out as he pedaled. His elbows flapped too, giving him the aspect of a prehistoric bird attempting liftoff.

But he got the hang of it, the motion of the bike creating its own delicious breeze. The sun was low; light slanted through and underneath the canopies of dracaenas and palms. The streets were cooling except in little patches where glare was reflected from hot parked cars; on a bike, the feel and smell of the air changed with every second. By the time Jake reached the big hotel he was feeling almost giddy with the pleasure of the changes.

Even so, his meeting with Quentin Dole got off to a rather rocky start.

He'd been shown to the producer's table in the Terrace Bar; it was an excellent table, on the rail overlooking the ocean and the sunset. Dole had risen affably to shake his hand. They'd agreed on what to drink—Tanqueray martinis. And, since they were near- contemporaries, the small talk came quite easily.

But then, midway through the first cocktail, the producer said, "So, Jake, d'you bring the outline?"

"Outline?"

At this one word answer, Dole seemed just a bit nonplussed. The sun was about a palm's breadth above the horizon; it kept slipping in and out among slabs of yellow cloud, and the lenses of the producer's glasses kept getting darker and lighter, lighter and darker. He said, "The network wants an outline. Your agent didn't tell you?"

Jake sucked his olive off its toothpick. It sent a tickling squirt of liquor down his throat. "Nobody said anything about an outline."

Dole still looked affable but he couldn't mask just a hint of a frown. "Hm, that's really not so good."

Jake shrugged. "I never do an outline. What's the point?"

The producer quietly held his ground. "The network wants an outline. They need something to approve."

The writer smiled but his resistance was rising and the smile looked tight. "Look, I've got ten weeks to write a book. Who's got time to cock around with an outline?"

The producer tried to smile back. His didn't quite work either. "It's how they operate. They need something to sign off on. Doesn't mean we're locked into it. If it changes, it changes."

"Then why bother doing it?"

The two men stared at each other over the rims of their martini glasses, their parallel and polite slow burns advancing by the finest of calibrations. Perhaps it was inevitable that there'd be some head-butting between them. A primal thing, a guy thing, a mutual testing that could lead either to friendship or to warfare. Dole, of course, was the richer and more powerful of the two men, but that was not always an advantage. Jake had the occasionally useful leverage of the free-lance, the unattached, the one with less to lose.

It made for a delicate standoff, and Dole decided to try a different tack. He said, "The network owns your publisher."

Jake curled his lips dismissively. "That could change any day and it really isn't my problem."

Realizing that his gambit had been ill-advised, the producer followed it up with yet another approach. With an ever more taut smile pulling at his face, trying to make the comment seem like half a compliment, he said, "You're a stubborn son of a bitch, aren't you?"

"About most things, no," Jake said. "About my work, yes." Then he added his own barb cloaked in the guise of grudging admiration. "And maybe you're a little too used to dealing with L.A. suck-ups who'll bend over and do whatever you tell them to."

At that, Dole swept off his glasses and rubbed the bridge of his nose. His companion's face hidden, Jake had no idea what was coming next. A punch? A thrown drink? A flipping of the table? Instead, Dole took a moment to regroup then shook his head and laughed. "All right, all right. Now that we know each other a little bit, how about we please start over? Let's have another drink."

He signaled for the waiter, and when the fresh cocktails arrived the two men made a conciliatory clink with their glasses. The producer said, "Okay, there's no outline. So how do *you* want to do this book?"

"For starters, I just need you to tell me what you want."

"What I want?"

"You want a murder mystery? More of a corporate sabotage kind of thing? Government conspiracies? Global cover-up? A prequel? A sequel? Some combination of all of the above?"

"Christ, Jake, it isn't like ordering Chinese food."

"Yes it is. In fact it's a lot like ordering Chinese food. A little of this, a little of that. I know the recipes. What I need from you are the ingredients."

"Go on."

"You want a tie-in, right? A story connected to the show, but not too much. Little strands. Teases. Coincidences. I get it. I can do that. But I need more to go on. I've only had time to watch the first half-dozen episodes."

This was a fib. He'd only watched three and a half.

"What did you think of them?" Dole asked.

What did he think? He thought they were utterly preposterous and highly annoying but drew the line at saying so. "Good soap opera…"

The producer didn't wince, and Jake went on.

"…catchy sub-plots, plenty of balls in the air. But I need to know what happens the rest of the season, the season or two after—"

Jake broke off because his tablemate suddenly seemed uncomfortable in the extreme. He'd lowered his head and was peeking somewhat spasmodically around him as if afraid that someone might be listening. Speaking barely above a whisper, he said, "Jake, we off the record here?"

"Of course. And even if we weren't, I'm just the writer, no one talks to me."

"Seriously now. Off the record?"

Jake nodded.

"Okay, then. Listen, I have no idea what happens in the next season or two. I have no idea what happens in the next *month* or two. I have three scripts in hand. After that…?" He let the question hang.

Jake took a moment to process it. Then he said, "The buzz is that the show will run for six or seven seasons."

"Right," said Dole. "And there are millions of people glued to their sets every week, dying to see how it all turns out, believing that there has to be a master plan, a God almost. But there's no master plan. There's no plan at all."

The producer swigged his drink, then leaned in closer, more confiding and seemingly more tipsy than he'd been just a moment before. They were three thousand miles from L.A. and he seemed relieved to talk. He took his glasses off and showed his eyes. What was in them wasn't fear exactly, but a kind of surprise and bewilderment, a silent but frank admission that he was in the middle of something that had gotten way too big for him, maybe too big for anybody.

"Last year," he went on, "me and some buddies sat down with a yellow pad and many bottles of Cabernet. We had this kick-ass idea for a pilot. That was it. Now we've got a monster hit, a cult, and I have no fucking clue where it's going."

Jake ate his second olive, scratched his nose, and said, "Be careful what you wish for, right? Must be a lot of pressure."

"Pressure," the producer echoed. "Put it this way. The show stays on track, I'm set for life, I write my own ticket. It tanks after a start like this, I probably never get a job again. The phone doesn't ring, the calls don't get returned, I'm dead. I don't think there's any middle ground."

He drummed his fingers on the table. Jake looked off at the ocean. The seam between the sea and sky was fading, the air and water both trending toward a violet that seemed to have no surface, only depth.

Rather jumpily, the producer flagged the waiter for another round. Then he pulled in a quick breath like he was trying to suck back the words he'd indulged himself by confiding. "This conversation, it never happened, right?"

"Scout's honor," Jake said. "Trust me."

Dole managed a grim laugh. "Which is how they say fuck you in Hollywood. Last two words I wanted to hear."

"Except we're not in Hollywood," said Jake, "and I mean it. It's between us. I appreciate your telling me. Now let's talk story."

7

Wobbling and weaving through mostly empty streets, Jake somehow made it home that evening. He opened the compound gate, rolled his bike into the rack, and was walking a bit unsteadily up the gravel path when he noticed a naked woman swimming laps.

The small pool wasn't really suitable for laps; it was only long enough for five, six strokes before a turn was called for; the laps, in fact, were as much about somersaults as swimming. Still, the naked woman determinedly shuttled back and forth, back and forth. A gibbous moon was high in the sky; it lit her tenderly and beautifully. There were highlights on the finely stranded muscles of her neck and shoulders. Her buttocks softly shone like a pair of wave-washed rocks just above the tide line. There was a playful frenzy in the foam that fizzed around her kicking feet, and when she twirled and dove, pushing off to change direction, he could sense the power in her thighs. Transfixed, he watched her do perhaps a half dozen circuits before she surfaced and looked up at him.

"Take a picture," she said. "It lasts longer."

Caught, Jake mumbled, "Sorry. Was I staring? Sorry. I think I've had a lot to drink."

Standing now, the water encircling her breasts like a shimmering blue bodice, the woman shook her hair and tried to clear an ear. Then she splayed her elbows along the apron of the pool. "Hey, no problem. If I was shy about being looked at I'd probably spend less time naked in public places. You new here?"

"As of today."

"Vacation?"

"No, not really. Working."

"Ah. You with the show?"

"*Adrift?*"

"Is there another one? You must be one of the unimportant people."

"Excuse me?"

"You're here. Like me. The stars, the bigshots, they get put up in fancy hotels and brought to the set in limos. I go in a minibus with the crew. What's your deal?"

"I'm writing a book for them."

"Ah, a brainy guy."

"I wouldn't jump to that conclusion."

"Me, I do stunts. That's why I'm out here swimming fucking laps when I could be in a nice bar drinking margaritas. I have a scene tomorrow. A big swim. I double for this bitch of a star. It's the worst job in the world but it's better than nothing. Would you reach me that towel over there?"

Jake grabbed the towel from a nearby lounge chair. It had a blue background with a big picture of a pink flamingo on it. With no shred of inhibition, the woman, leggy as a model but with the firm and straight-hipped step of an athlete, climbed out of the pool and began to dry herself. Her brown hair was shiny with wet and wild from the somersaults. Her young face was open and pleasant but a bit too rough-hewn to be really pretty, the nose a shade too broad, the cheekbones a little too flat. She twisted the towel around her torso so that the flamingo's beak seemed to be reaching down between her breasts. Then she lay down on the lounge and took a cigarette from a pack on a plastic table.

Reading Jake's face, she said, "I know, I know. Smoking. Right after a workout, no less. Girl can't be good all the time. Want one?"

He declined. The woman patted a chair next to her and invited him to sit. "Let's chat a while. It's so damn quiet here. I thought Key West was a party town. So where's the freakin' party? I'd rather be downtown, you know, Duval Street and all, but beggars can't be choosers, right? I'm Donna." She extended a hand that was still cool and a little crinkled from the pool.

"I'm Jake. Nice to see you. Meet you, I mean." He couldn't quite forget that she was nude underneath the towel and this made it a little difficult to pursue a normal conversation. Somewhat awkwardly, he said, "I always thought being a stunt person would be a really cool job."

Donna smoked her cigarette. "Yeah. Lacerations, broken bones, it's great. It's just that this particular gig happens to suck."

"What's so bad about it?"

She blew some smoke out with a quiet fury. "What's so bad about it. Well, for starters, I'm a distant second banana to a princess who doesn't like to get wet and doesn't like to get dirty. So why's she doing a show where the whole fucking thing is about water and muck? Next thing–our character's a real superwoman. She can do anything, fix anything, she's always showing up the guys. So whenever there's something super to be done, that's me up there. But that's all I get to do: be super. She gets to be the actual woman. She gets to act. I get to grunt now and then. She gets the close-ups, I get the crotch shots while I'm climbing up a tree. Not to mention she makes fifty or a hundred times more money. The whole thing's so fucked up."

Jake looked for something to say but he was pressed back in his chair by Donna's virulence.

"Hey," she went on, "she's prettier than I am. I know that. I got eyes. But I don't miss by much. A little knife-work, a little collagen. You think I miss by much?"

Jake swallowed. "Actually, I think you're great-looking."

"Great-looking. Okay. Not as good as beautiful, but I'll take it, thanks."

She stubbed out her cigarette and turned over on her side. The towel followed her but not precisely. Lifting on an elbow, fixing Jake with a ferocious gaze, she went on. "It's just that I'd be so much better in that part. I know that character inside and out. I *am* that character. When she's treated like a girl, she gets pissed off and has to show how tough she is. When her toughness pushes people away, she wants to get all soft and be treated like a girl. She's stuck in this pattern. Tomboy, pussycat. Pussycat, ballbuster. Back to pussycat, back to tomboy. I get it. I could play every little shred of it. I could win a fucking Emmy in that role."

Trying to be helpful, Jake said, "Maybe you'll get to play a part like that sometime."

She picked a fleck of tobacco from her tongue and pushed forth a dismissive sound. "Fat chance. You don't go from stunt girl to leading lady. That would take a miracle. And I happen not to believe in miracles. Except maybe the do-it-yourself kind. So there it is. But hey, you shouldn't have to listen to me bitch all night. Tell me about you, what you're doing here, your book. It's about the show?"

Jake leaned his head back and looked up at the stars. "Sort of. Not really. Yes and no."

"That clears it up," said Donna.

"You know Quentin Dole?"

"Christ, that's like asking if I know the Pope. He's the man. He's the franchise. They say he's a genius. Has the whole series mapped out in his head."

"We just had drinks—"

"You had drinks with Quentin? So you're a bigshot after all."

"Not hardly. But we had drinks, we chatted, we're trying to figure out what the book should be."

"Drinks with Quentin," Donna said again. "You're a bigshot but you hide it. I think that's nice."

"Stop, please. But I have a question for you. Would you rather not ride the minibus tomorrow morning? Quentin's sending a car to bring me to the set."

"A limo? That's more like it."

"I doubt it. Just a car."

"Still beats the hell out of a minibus. I have to do anything to get this ride?"

"Excuse me?"

"You know. *Do* anything. I mean, this is show business, after all."

33

Slightly embarrassed, not sure if he was coming across more as a prude or more as a cad, Jake said, "No. No, nothing like that."

"See, you're a nice guy. I could see right off you are."

"Just be ready by eight."

"I'll be ready by seven," she said. "Getting into character, you know." And she gave a little laugh that dissolved in the blue haze above the pool.

8

Donna, all revved up, was awake at dawn and soon got down to her daily regimen of stretching and core work. By seven she was showered and dressed and rubbed with lotions that made her taut skin glisten. But then her morning had a setback. She couldn't find the looseleaf binder that held her scripts. She was sure she'd left it on the wicker table in her tiny living room. Well, almost sure. Occasionally she read scripts out by the pool, fantasizing that some talent scout or bigshot might happen by and be fascinated. Or sometimes she read scenes aloud in the bathtub, playing all the parts, sloshing water as she gestured. Still, there were only so many places the notebook could be, and it didn't seem to be in any of them. This embarrassed her. Even though she had no lines, it seemed unprofessional to show up on set without her script. She looked for it again and again.

Jake, slightly hung over, slept till twenty of eight. He made coffee, stuck his head under running water, pulled on the first clothes he found. He wasn't very talkative in the morning.

Their ride in fact was not a limo but at least it was a black Town Car and at least the driver, while not in uniform, wore a jaunty cap. He drove them through the sleepy pastel streets of Old Town, only the cats apparently awake, then north on Highway 1, through precincts where Key West ceased being special and looked a lot like many other slightly seamy tourist towns—here a pancake house, there a porn shop, a grim line of motels that had lost some paint on their archways and some letters from their signs.

Not till they turned off the highway at a place called Big Sandy Key did the landscape once again seem singular, antic, a somehow facetious version of reality stuck onto the wider world with a piece of fraying tape. For one thing, the name Big Sandy was either a willful illusion, a developer's fib, or a mapmaker's joke: there wasn't any sand there. There was only coral, chunks of it in every size. Slabs big enough to serve as pockmarked driveways. Outcrops that broke toes in the dark. Gravel that ranged from knucklebone size down to something almost like dust but with very sharp edges. Through this finer stuff, mangroves grew, their arched roots standing in the water, capturing muck.

An untidy democracy held sway on Big Sandy Key. Just where the paved road ended there were random scraggles of trailer parks. Then, farther on, where the sharp gray weeds gave place to pampered bougainvillea, the second or third homes of millionaires sprawled under their blue or green roofs along inlets and canals. Farther on again, where the island sloped almost imperceptibly back toward the mangroves, there were glorified shacks on cinderblock stilts, ugly but serviceable perches where tattooed families could watch floods go by while drinking beer and eating shrimp.

Where even the gravel road finally gave out, there was a dusty clearing with a wooden dock that did not inspire confidence. Its pilings leaned and snaggled like teeth in need of braces; its planks were scarred with rot and there were knotholes where the light shone through. In front of this dock the crew's minibus was stopped; eight or ten large fellows were unpacking gear.

Donna, who'd been surprisingly silent the entire ride, now leaned forward and said to the driver, "Pull up close. I want those jerkoffs to see me arrive. And if you don't mind, open my door for me. Hold my fingertips as I step out. I'll slip you ten bucks. I want it to be like I'm at the fucking Oscars."

Heads turned as Donna made her entrance. Jake unfolded his long body from the seat and, uninvited, she quickly and firmly took his arm, not the elbow but the whole arm, clutching it with both her hands and holding it tight against her side. She tugged on his shoulder to bring his ear down close to her. "I know what those pissants are thinking. They're sure I must've fucked you last night. Just to pay the fare. Why spoil their fun? Let 'em think it. Besides, I like holding your arm. It's a little skinny but I like it."

They rode the funky pontoon barge across the channel, maybe a quarter mile wide, that separated Big Sandy from the largest of its three outlying and usually uninhabited islets. On the other side, Donna was quickly shepherded off to be made up and dressed, giving Jake's arm a final and rather proprietary squeeze before she moved away.

At that moment the writer was approached by a woman with a clipboard.

She had very green eyes, peachy skin, and short reddish hair; she wore no-nonsense khaki shorts and a white fishing shirt with long sleeves and lots of little pockets. Through the bustle all around her, she radiated calm—one of those people who was always busy and never in a hurry. Extending a hand, she introduced herself as Claire Segal. "Quentin asked me to show you around," she said. Then, with a brief but pointed glance at Donna's retreating backside, she asked if he was enjoying Key West so far.

"Yeah, fine," he said. "I haven't had time to see much of it yet."

"Apparently not."

A little slow on the uptake, Jake finally caught the innuendo. "Donna? Hey, she's way too young for me."

Now it was Claire who needed an instant to respond. "Too young? Wow. Did I just hear those words? From a man?"

"Guess you're from L.A. Besides, you're giving me way too much credit. I don't move that fast. Never have."

"TV speeds things up," said Claire. "Everything."

"We met around the pool. I offered her a lift, that's all."

"Whatever. Let's not gossip. I understand you don't do outlines."

He scratched an ear. "No."

She looked at his hands, empty of pen or paper or laptop or iPad. "I see you don't take notes either."

"No."

"You're sort of casual about all this."

"Yes."

She cocked her head at a *who-is-this-guy?* sort of angle then nodded. "Okay. Come on, I'll show you how we film *Adrift.*"

She led him to a sort of souped-up golf cart with oversized tires and they set out over the knobby coral. The islet rose in a very shallow dome topped by a cluster of casuarinas whose wispy leaves filtered the hot light like the glass of a cathedral. Then, on the far side, it sloped through sedges to a shoreline that could have been five thousand miles from anywhere. Two smaller islets lay beyond; the waters between them were emerald green in the shallows and a stunning turquoise where the channels deepened. There were eddies around the roots of mangroves; the eddies were the only evidence of movement in a world suddenly silent and still. Nothing man-made was visible for as far as the eye could see.

"*Voila,*" said Claire. "Our miniature universe. Took weeks of scouting to find it, but it's pretty perfect. We get sunrise and sunset. There's places for campfires, trysts, fistfights, conspiracies. If we bring in bad guys or cannibals or ghouls—"

"Are you?" Jake cut in.

"Are we what?"

"Bringing in cannibals or ghouls."

Claire gave a rather coy shrug. "Hey, you're the one who had three martinis with Quentin."

"And you're the one who's out here every day."

"Putting on band-aids," said Claire. "Watching the clock with the union guys. I do the detail stuff, the nitty-gritty. The grand overarching vision—that's Quentin's department."

"Grand overarching vision," Jake repeated, spreading his hands to frame the words. "Do I detect just a whiff of sarcasm?"

Claire looked at him sideways, didn't quite wink but sent a tilted smile that was halfway to a wink, and left it at that.

A soft splashing was heard offshore, and when Jake and Claire broke off their gaze they saw a fellow rowing a dinghy into the channel between the islets. When he'd made it to the turquoise water in the middle, he boated his oars then reached down between his feet and lifted an enormous lobster. The beast must have been four feet across. Its claws jabbed and pinched the air and its tail curled and humped in a manner that was quite obscene. The fellow threw it overboard. It sank, trailing an almost invisible tiny buoy that now bobbed on the surface.

"Mechanical," said Claire. "Pretty realistic, no? It's for your girl-friend's big scene."

"She's not my girlfriend."

"You keep saying that. Let's get over to the set."

9

Up over the next hump in the coral, the cast and crew had gathered. Fat cameramen with their shirt-tails out were setting up their angles. Assistants were placing scrims in trees to soften the sunlight, stylists were spraying shine on hair.

Rob Stanton, the director, was pacing in front of the group and saying, "Okay folks, so this is where we are. The meeting scene has broken up. Dismal failure. No one could agree on anything. So much for democracy.

"Now we have a two-scene between Lulu and Tony. Lovers for three episodes, but everyone in America knows it can't last. Tony's too passive, cerebral. Lulu's all action, impulse. This scene is where it really comes to a head. We ready?"

The two actors stepped out of the group into a small clearing near the shoreline. The one who played Tony didn't really look all that cerebral, at least not without a shirt on. He had a V-shaped torso, rippling abs, a jaw so square it would have sat up on a table. He wore tight jeans that were held up, sort of, by an impromptu belt made of salvaged rope. As for Candace, she looked ravishing in a faded blue cambric shirt with torn sleeves and a plunging neckline, its tails tied off snugly, liftingly, at the midriff. She wore tiny yellow shorts that exposed a delectable crescent of flesh just at the cusp between leg and buttock. A nice S&M touch had been added in the form of a painted-on wound on the left side of her neck.

Claire, standing off to the side with Jake, handed him her copy of the script. "It isn't Chekhov but you can read along."

Cameras came up to speed. Microphone booms dangled overhead. The director called for action.

LULU

My God, you were such a wimp
in there!

TONY

A wimp? Why? Because I didn't scream
my head off? Because I let other people talk?

LULU

Talk. Right. Talk, talk, talk. That's all you
do is talk. We're not gonna get ourselves
out of here by talking.

TONY

No? How then? By being completely negative
about everything?

LULU

Negative? I'm not negative. I'm realistic.
I deal with things.

TONY

So do I. In my way. Look, I try to be fair—

LULU

Fair? You can't eat fair. We don't need a
goddam committee. We don't need a freakin'
Constitution. We need food.

TONY

Agreed. And the best way to get it—

LULU

–is to shut up and go get it!

Lulu furiously wheels and races full-speed toward the water.

Except Candace didn't race toward the water. She turned, flashed a last contemptuous look back at Tony, took a single step, and broke the scene. The director called, "Cut."

After a moment to exhale, he said, "Candace, dear, the script says you run full-speed toward the water."

The actress pointed at the sharp and gnarly excuse for a beach. "I'm not running on that shit. I'll cut my feet."

"The running is the climax of the scene."

"No, my last look back is the climax. I hope you got it good and close. Let Donna do the running."

The director squeezed his lips together and looked over at Claire. Claire looked over at the cameraman. The cameraman looked up from his monitor and nodded discreetly. Sighing, the director said, "Okay, we'll leave it there for now. We'll pick up with the running. Donna ready?"

Donna was. Donna was always ready. She was always ready ahead of time and always as eager to get started as a jumpy thoroughbred.

Now she stepped out of the cluster of casuarinas just as Candace was slipping back toward it. For an instant Jake thought he must be looking at clones. Donna was wearing an identical blue shirt, tied off in the same bust-enhancing way. She had the same tiny yellow shorts that revealed a remarkably similar sliver of behind. Her slightly dull brown hair had been tucked under a shining black wig; the left side of her neck, the twin of Candace's, sported an oddly becoming painted-on wound.

She strode to the spot where the star had last been standing. She took a couple of deep breaths, stared at the ground in front of her to gather focus. She tried not to notice that cast and crew who weren't involved in the shot had wandered unceremoniously off. This was just a little swimming scene, a throwaway. Just the stunt girl.

The director called for action.

Donna wheeled and ran. She ran low, like an Indian scout, slightly bent at the waist, arms compact at her sides. Coral shards flew from her heels and when she reached the water's edge she took a final lunging stride that flattened into a perfect shallow dive. Seamlessly, the dive turned into swimming, hands cupping the water, feet churning the foam. Strong shoulders lifted the determined arms, breaths came in quick but measured sips between the strokes. Distance stretched between Donna and the shore as sunshine put hot white spangles on the broken water.

It was the sound man who first noticed something wrong. A low rumble coming through his headset, very faint at the beginning, something felt as much as heard but gradually rising in both pitch and volume. He tried without success to catch the director's eye.

Donna tirelessly swam, the rhythm steady, the kick unflagging.

The sound man waved a hand as the low rumble was rising toward something like a mechanical growl. No one saw him waving.

Donna swam.

She'd almost reached the tiny buoy when the speedboat— enormous, gleaming, up on plane at a ferocious angle like a breaching orca—came tearing around the far side of the islet, peeling toward the channel at breakneck speed. She didn't see it. If she heard it, she paid no mind. This was her scene. The big swim. Through the pellucid water she finally saw the mechanical lobster wriggling on a patch of sand a dozen feet below. She pulled in breath, arced her body, the deep dive smooth and streamlined from all those somersaults in the pool, and headed down to grab the prize.

On shore, people were frantically waving and screaming now. They windmilled their arms at the unheeding speedboat. They shouted to Donna who had no chance of hearing them. Helplessly, pinned between quailing hope and sick certainty, they watched the distance disappear between the careening boat and the place where the stunt girl would surface.

She came up, facing shore, a smile barely visible, waving the lobster in triumph for just an instant before the speedboat ran her over.

The planing hull barely grazed her neck and shoulders, almost gave her time to dive away from harm. But the propeller shafts caught her as she tried to sink to safety. One shaft slammed into her shoulder, wrenching it at a grotesque angle in its socket. The other nailed her at the bottom of her ribcage, the propeller biting into the flesh of her side as it raked past.

At the spot where Donna had last been seen a slick of red appeared in the turquoise water and the speedboat rocketed away without ever slowing down.

PART 2

10

Jake found himself in the water, clothes on, sneakers on, first wading then swimming, surrounded by twenty other flailing people who were trying clumsily, desperately, to help. It could have been a scene from the pilot of *Adrift*, people clawing at the sea with looks of horror on their faces. A better swimmer got to Donna first and dragged the limp body ashore; it left behind it a meandering zag of blood.

It was impossible to tell if Donna was alive or dead. Her right shoulder was hunched up much too high; the arm seemed stuck in an ungainly position, as if she was about to serve a tennis ball. The salt water had mostly stanched the bleeding from her appalling wound, but the torn flesh had an oozing sheen to it, a sheen like that of defrosting beef. Someone who knew CPR took charge. He turned Donna's head sideways and pressed lightly on her belly. Pink water, an intermittent stream of it, as from a faulty pump, spilled from her nose and mouth. He cleared her tongue, pinched her nostrils, and starting breathing his own air down into her lungs.

After a while, her eyes very briefly opened, a single cough wracked her, and she gurgled out something that sounded like *Fuck happened?* Then she either passed out again or died.

In minutes a helicopter appeared. Riding pontoons, it landed in the shallows and dispatched two men and a stretcher. They carefully maneuvered the motionless Donna onto it and flew away.

Once the engine noise had faded there was a shocked and shamefaced silence around the set. People had a hard time meeting one another's eyes. The cast and crew seemed in the grip of an obscure, unfocused guilt, as if they secretly believed that, by their lack of interest in Donna's big scene and in Donna herself, they had somehow conspired in the calamity, tossed her away as a sacrifice. Cameras sat idle, lenses cast down. Lights and scrims hung forgotten in trees like pieces of last year's Halloween display.

The Marine Patrol arrived, then the cops. They started asking questions, and the queasy silence was replaced by a chorus of nervous, staccato answers, people jumping at the chance to speak, to purge themselves of what they'd seen. But it turned out they had almost nothing of use to say. The incident had been filmed, correct? Well, actually, it hadn't been. It *should* have been, but it wasn't. Only a single camera had been trained on Donna as she swam. The cameraman, knowing that the take was ruined when he saw the sound man toss aside his headset, then catching the general panic as the boat wheeled into the channel, had abandoned his post to join in the futile waving and shouting. The camera had pivoted, capturing serenely useless images of blank horizon and innocent sky.

That left eyewitness accounts, and it turned out that, in the rush and terror of the moment, no two people had seen the exact same thing. The most basic details were a muddle. What color was the speedboat? Some people thought the hull was black, some remembered it as dark blue or green. Some people recalled an open cockpit and a windshield, others thought the cabin was enclosed. Some people had seen a lone man at the wheel; some thought they'd seen a pair of men, and others had seen no one on the boat at all. Did the boat ever seem to be intentionally steering toward the victim? No one could say one way or the other. Did it seem at any point, before or after the collision, to slow down? That was the one thing everyone agreed about. The craft had never slowed.

The cops left. The silence returned. The cameraman who'd failed to shoot the scene busied himself with trivial tasks and tried to disappear. People wandered, paced. No one quite knew what to do with the rest of the morning. After a brief and awkward time, Jake told Claire he had to leave.

He took the barge across to Big Sandy Key to meet the driver with the black Town Car. Seeing him alone, the driver said, "Holy shit. That chick they med-evac'd. Was that your girlfriend?"

"She's not my girlfriend. Where's the hospital?"

At the front desk of Florida Keys General, the switchboard was flashing and the receptionist was frazzled. No, there was no information available on Donna Alvarez. No, she had no idea when there would be. No, there was no one else he could speak with at this time. He was welcome to wait in the lobby but she really saw no point in it. Information would be made public as it came available. She had no other advice, she had to pick up on a call.

For a few minutes Jake paced through the lobby, slaloming around the potted palms, his feet still squishing in his sodden sneakers. Belatedly, it occurred to him to wonder why he'd gone to the hospital at all. He and Donna were mere acquaintances. And he was, generally speaking, a rather aloof sort of person, a watcher, a teller of stories rather than a participant in them. So why was he getting involved? The best he could come up with was that he didn't seem to have a choice. You didn't always get to pick the people or events you cared about. Sometimes things just happened. You started as a mere bystander, a chance witness, nothing more. Then, either suddenly or by slow degrees, you noticed you'd been tricked out of your detachment, you'd crossed a line and actually gave a shit how this thing turned out. Why? Simple decency? Idle curiosity? Or was it just that the bad luck of witnessing a train wreck conferred responsibility, imposed a connection it would be shameful or impossible to dodge?

He took another run at the receptionist and got nothing. Finally he gave up and went back to the compound. It was barely noon but it felt much later. He hadn't yet spent twenty-four hours in Key West. Way too much had happened.

He pushed open the compound gate and found Joey Goldman sitting by the pool. Sitting, but not relaxing; he kicked his feet out, pulled them back, kept rearranging his elbows. He said to Jake, "Helluva thing, huh?"

"You've heard?"

"It's all over local news already. I mean, come on, it's show business. I came down to check on Donna's place, see if there was anything I could do."

Jake said, "I just came from the hospital."

"Nice of you to go. You see her?"

"See her? I don't even know if she's alive."

Joey blinked. "They didn't tell you?"

"Tell me what?"

"She's in the I.C.U. Serious condition, just down from critical. Expected to recover. It was on the radio like ten minutes ago."

Jake felt his face get instantly hot, the skin congested. His eyes burned and welled up. This was from relief but he chose to ascribe it to fury. "Fuck! They won't tell me anything while I'm standing in the lobby but they'll put it on the radio?"

"Crappy hospital," said Joey. "They shoulda took her to Miami. She was a star, that's where they woulda took her. You saw it happen?"

"Yeah. It was nasty." Jake blew out a deep breath. It suddenly seemed like it had been a while since he'd used his lungs. Inhaling, he remembered the taste of the air, flowery and salty. He sat down in a chair near Joey's.

Joey said, "The cops are calling it an accident. That's their way of saying the victim was an out-of-towner and they don't wanna be bothered."

Jake said nothing.

"It look like an accident to you?"

The writer fumbled for an answer. Until that moment it hadn't really occurred to him that the disaster could have been anything else. The possibility put a sick taste at the back of his throat. "I…I don't know," he said. "People like to go too fast in boats, right? That adrenaline thing. Plus, the way those crazy speedboats ride so high, I can't figure how anyone sees what's out in front of him. Happened so fast, maybe the guy didn't even know he'd hit anything."

"He'd've felt a bump," said Joey. "Could've been bottom. Could've been a big ray or a manatee. Next time the guy turns on a radio or television, he'll know what he hit. Then we'll see what happens. My guess: nothing."

Jake looked down at the pool and had a brief, lovely, and disturbing vision of Donna swimming in it. He blinked it away. "Nothing?"

"Think about it," Joey said. "Say it was an accident. Totally innocent. Now it's a hit-and-run. The guy's gonna turn himself in? What if he was hopped up, drunk, in the middle of a blowjob? What if it was someone's kid out for a joy ride? Forget the criminal part, just look at the liability. I just don't see somebody coming forward." He paused, rearranged his restless feet. "Even if it was an accident."

Jake looked sideways at Joey. "But you don't really think it was." He didn't put it as a question.

Joey shrugged. "Hey, wha' do I know? Very little. But I've lived down here a long time and I know there are a lot of bad people doing a lot of bad things with very fast boats. Running drugs, running guns, smuggling people. And usually not getting caught. That fucking boat could be anywhere by now. Miami. Cuba. The Bahamas. Or tucked into some mangroves right under our noses."

Jake still resisted the idea of murderous intent. It just distressed and offended him too much. "Why would someone want to hurt her?"

"I'm not saying someone does. I'm just saying we may never know. Happens a lot down here. Weird shit happens and stays weird. Eventually people lose interest or forget. Or get paid off to forget. That's just how it goes."

There was a silence. The palm fronds waved and scratched. A faint whiff of chlorine spun up from the pool.

Jake said, "D'you know her very well?"

"Well? Not really. But she's been here almost three months, off and on, whenever they've been shooting. Usually on her own. At the start there was a guy with her some of the time. Haven't seen him lately. I think she threw him out a month or so ago. Just as well. Struck me as a knucklehead, maybe worse. But her I like. A little crazy, I think, but a pistol."

"Yeah, she is. Both."

Jake looked away and Joey took the opportunity to send him an appraising glance. The new arrival looked fairly ragged, beat up, overwhelmed; Joey felt bad for him and wanted to do him a kindness. Rising from his chair, he said, "You happen to be free for dinner?"

Jake just blinked.

"Tell you what. Why don't you come by later and eat with us. Me, my wife, an old friend."

Touched, surprised, Jake said, "Jeez, that's really nice but—"

"Come on. We'll drink some wine, we'll toast to Donna's health. You'll feel better being with some people." He glanced toward the stunt girl's empty cottage. "Little too quiet around here today. Come by around six. Twelve-fourteen White Street, two blocks before the pier."

11

At a private marina on an exclusive island in Biscayne Bay, a gleaming speedboat was being carefully tied into its berth.

The boat's color was a mysteriously shimmering purplish gray, easily mistaken for blue or black. Its steeply raked and mirror-tinted windshield was seamlessly joined to a fixed bimini that made the cockpit appear, from various angles, either open or closed. There was something shark-like in the tumescent bulge of the hull. The custom craft was on the one hand very distinctive and on the other hand a numb amalgam of the many hundreds of fast, loud, expensive and dangerous toys that plied the waters of the Gulf Stream and the Florida Straits.

When the last dock line had been cleated off, a big man stepped from the boat, eschewing the offered gangway in favor a single, long, thick-legged but athletic step to shore. Reaching into a pocket of his tight black shorts, he produced a wad of bills and peeled off a fifty for the wiry Spanish guys who manned the ropes. Then he headed toward land, where a rank of condos rose like abrupt glass buttes in a landscape that was otherwise astonishingly flat.

Seen from behind, the big man was a series of hard angles and lumpy curves. His short black hair was clipped knife-straight across his neck; muscles bulged in his shoulders like the knobs in braided bread. His hips were square and narrow but his rounded buttocks flinched inside his too-tight shorts, pulling the seam into his buttcrack, forcing him to kick out and shake a foot every third step to clear it.

He walked over to a high-rise whose pretentious porte-cochere was mere yards from the softly lapping bay. He gave his name to a surly doorman and was shown up to the twenty-second floor. Not to an apartment on the twenty-second floor—to the entire level of the building. He was met at the elevator by a bodyguard even beefier than himself. The two giants greeted one another with a light bump of their enormous fists, then the visitor was ushered into the sprawling apartment.

In the living room he was briefly blinded by the glare of the unshaded windows, behind which the view was so large you could see the curving of the earth. Yachts, fishing skiffs, cabin cruisers inched along the water, leaving tiny chevron wakes like toy craft in a park pond. As his eyes adjusted, he saw a short man sitting on a sofa, one arm circling behind as though staking claim to some babe. He was short but not small; he had a thick neck that seemed to have been hammered down into his wide shoulders and a barrel chest that stretched the buttons of his patterned shirt. He said, "So?"

By way of answer, the visitor reached into his shorts and produced the ignition key for the speedboat. The short man raised a hand and he tossed the key to him.

"Ya have the class to gas it up at least?"

"To the brim," the big man said.

"It's clean?"

"Washed and buffed at the gas dock. Those spicks are pretty good." There was a brief silence, then he added, "Don't worry, no problem, everything went fine. Just a little something I had to do."

The short man stopped him with a gesture. "Don't tell me how it went. Don't tell me where you went. Don't tell me what you did. It's got nothing to do with me. You asked me to loan you the boat, I loaned you the boat. I did you a favor. There's any headaches, I report it stolen and it's your ass that's in a sling."

"I get it. That's the deal."

"And inna meantime, you owe me. Don't forget that. Don't make me remind you."

He ended the meeting by looking away. That was all it took, just a shift in his glance. The big man left, discreetly kicking at his too-tight shorts as he walked.

12

Jake, wrung out, had slept an hour in the middle of the day. When he woke up he decided to have a swim. He wasn't much of a swimmer but suddenly he felt like doing a few laps. He realized only dimly that this was a sort of mute *homage* to Donna. Going native, he didn't bother with a bathing suit, just draped a towel around himself and headed outside.

Bryce was cleaning the pool when he got there. He was cleaning it with exquisite slowness. Actually, at the moment Jake first noticed him, he wasn't cleaning it at all, just standing on the tile apron, barefoot in his red sarong, holding the skimmer very still and at an angle from his body as though he was about to begin his approach to a pole vault. His eyes were dreamily focused on something in the water, a leaf that had wandered to the very edge of the tiny whirlpool created by the filter. It didn't quite get sucked in; it couldn't quite escape the pull. It inched away, spun, backslid, and then the little drama started all over. Bryce watched it for quite a while, wondered how long the suspense could possibly go on, what it would take to break the stalemate. Then he noticed Jake.

"Oh, hi," he said. "You want to go in?"

"I'll wait," Jake said. "No hurry. Finish what you're doing."

Rather wearily, Bryce said, "No, it's okay, I've done enough for now. I'll finish later. Go 'head, have your swim."

Jake felt suddenly bashful; New Yorkers, crammed in among eight million strangers, tended not to go naked, after all. Deferring the moment when he would drop his towel, he said, "You enjoy your swim yesterday?"

"Hmm?"

"That guy who threw you in the pool. I didn't see it but I heard the splash. Fun and games?"

Bryce shook his head with more sorrow than anger. "Oh, that guy. What a jerk. Donna's boyfriend."

"Boyfriend? Joey said she dumped him a month ago."

"Okay, old boyfriend. Good riddance. Talk about a toxic relationship. This was radioactive. Passionate, I guess, but really messy. I used to hear them arguing all the time."

Jake finally tossed away the towel and waded in. When he was solar plexus deep, his elbows held out like the wings of a chicken, Bryce continued, "Not that I was eavesdropping or anything. It's just that when the pool pump isn't running I hear everything. I'd hear them arguing, fucking, throwing things. Sometimes all at the same time."

Surprised at his own curiosity, Jake said, "So what did they argue about?"

Bryce shrugged. "Name it. Money. Jealousy. Who was flirting with who in some bar. Mostly her career, though. Just a lot of back-and-forth."

"Her career?"

Bryce laid the skimmer on the tiles and sat down on a lounge. A subtle but surprising change came over him. As if unconsciously, he began to play the mimic, started doing characters. Like a lot of passive people, he seemed to have a knack for this. "She complained a lot about her job. *I do all the work, I don't get the credit. No one even knows it's me up there!*"

Jake the ghostwriter glanced down at his chilled and shriveled pecker floating in the water. "Sometimes that's just how it goes."

"Right," said Bryce, "but the boyfriend, he's like sick of hearing it. Ya hate the work so much, why do it? And she's like, I don't hate the work. I love the work, ya moron, that's the problem. And he's like, That makes no sense to me. And she's like, Figures that it wouldn't. A little too complex. And he doesn't quite get that, so he starts in on something else. So why you don't stop bitching and let me help. She laughs. Help, right. He says, Like what if something happens to this other broad? She says, You know what? You're ridiculous. And back and forth and back and forth until finally they break up."

Standing in the pool, elbows spread out on the tiles, Jake said, "Wait a second. They broke up over *that?*"

"Over what?"

"Over him threatening the other actress."

Mildly, Bryce said, "Oh I don't think it was a real threat. Just beating his chest. He threatens everybody. That's what he does. Some people say hello. This guy says he'll break your legs."

"He threaten Donna when she dumped him?"

"Sure. Of course. All the usual drama, tough guy stuff. *You'll regret it. You'll be sorry—*"

He broke off abruptly because Jake's cell phone had started ringing. The phone was on a resonating metal table that made the ring seem very harsh and loud. Bryce started walking toward it and said to Jake, "You need to take that?"

Jake hesitated. He didn't want to take the call. He wanted to pursue the conversation. But before he could actually decide if he would take the call or not, Bryce had handed him the phone and he'd said hello.

It was Quentin Dole calling from L.A.

As encounters with Quentin almost always did, this one started pleasantly enough. "How are you, Jake?" he said.

There was seemingly genuine concern in his voice and Jake assumed this was in reference to what had happened to Donna. That would have been the natural thing, the human thing. Jake said, "Little upset, to tell the truth."

The answer, oddly, seemed to take the producer by surprise. He hesitated a moment, then said, "Yeah, yeah, it's terrible what happened. Awful. We've already got people working on it."

"Working on it?" Jake said. He was still standing in the chest-deep water. Bryce moved a discreet distance from the pool, not that he wasn't listening anyway.

"You know, managing it. Shaping the story. How it plays with the media. Our lead publicist should just be landing in Miami."

"Publicist? Quentin, this woman is really busted up. She could've died. Who knows what kind of recovery she'll make?"

"She'll be fine. She's union, she's got great insurance."

"This isn't about fucking insurance. It's about what happened to this person. And you have no idea if she'll be fine or not."

"You sound a little upset," the producer said.

"I just told you I'm upset. I guess you weren't listening."

"I guess I missed it. Sorry. But I wanted to talk to you about your book. I've had a few ideas."

"My book?"

"Remember," said Quentin, "when we were kicking things around, you mentioned a global conspiracy as one kind of story we might do? Well, I got back here and it clicked. There's this character, maybe he's a scientist, or a spy, or someone working for a really smart and radical Greenpeace kind of outfit. Something like that. And he stumbles onto something he's not supposed to know."

Jake had spun away from the edge of the pool and was pacing in slow motion through the water. "Quentin, I really don't want to talk about this now."

The producer went on as though he hadn't heard. "A new weapon. Being worked on not by any one country, but a whole group of countries. There's your global conspiracy angle, the paranoia angle: The governments know, the people don't know. Except this one guy finds out that the weapon is going to be tested. Where? In the middle of the ocean. And what happens with this weapon? It's so powerful that it basically cracks open the world. So you see where I'm going?"

Jake said, "I can't believe this is what you want to talk about. I just saw someone bleeding in the water, practically drowned. I can't think about this now."

"What it means," said Quentin Dole, "is that the tsunami that wrecked the cruise ship is just one piece of a much bigger puzzle, a much bigger disaster. And it raises the possibility—just a possibility, now, nothing made too definite—that our survivors, *if* they're alive, which of course has to stay an open question, are the last people alive on earth. Not too damn much chance of getting rescued then, right? So what do you think?"

"I think you're being a total insensitive dick."

That, the producer finally seemed to hear. He fell abruptly silent and Jake went on.

"Don't you even care what happened to this woman?"

"I care. Of course I care. We're all like family on this show."

"That's disgusting, putrid bullshit and you know it. Save it for the sound bites. You don't care at all. Admit it, at least."

Quentin Dole, as was his custom and his instinct when cornered, did not argue but sought to slip away along a different path. "Jake," he said, "can we please be a little professional here? We've got ten weeks to do a book. We can't afford to get all emotional and go on strike every time there's a little hiccup."

"A little hiccup? A member of your *family* gets chopped up by a speedboat and to you this is a little hiccup? That's fucked. That's really fucked."

He held the phone away as if it carried a disease and pushed the little red button. Pushing the little red button did not quite have the cathartic power of slamming down a receiver, but still, it was emphatic enough that Jake's hand trembled just a bit. He waded to the edge of the pool and slid the phone along the tiles. Then he submerged. Just sat down at the bottom to hide out for a moment.

When he surfaced Bryce was standing nearby. He said, "Well, I guess you told him."

Jake blinked chlorine from his eyes and glanced up at the sky. Gulls were wheeling, a squad of pelicans was scudding by. Sure enough, things were starting to look a little different here. What mattered, what didn't. What was bullshit, what was real. Suddenly pleased with himself, Jake said, "Yeah, I guess I did." And he slipped back underwater for a while.

13

Some minutes later, while he was drying off in caressing sunshine, Jake got another call. It was Claire Segal.

Seeming to savor the whole idea, she said, "I heard you just hung up on Quentin."

"He tells you everything?"

"Not hardly. He doesn't tell anybody everything. Did it feel good?"

"Hanging up? Yeah, it did."

"I'm envious. Anyway, he asked me to call to apologize."

Jake wasn't sure he'd heard right. Maybe he still had water in his ear. "Wait a second. I hung up on him. And he's the one apologizing?"

"That's right."

Disarmed, Jake fumbled for a moment then said, "Well, that's nice of him."

"No it isn't."

"It isn't?"

"It's pragmatic. Classic Quentin. He can't afford to piss you off."

"Still, to apologize—"

"What? It costs him nothing. He has no pride. No, that's not exactly right. He prides himself on getting what he needs from people. Doesn't matter how. Charm, threats, tantrums, apologies. He makes himself big or makes himself little. Whatever gets him where he needs to go."

Jake said, "I think you've just described a textbook sociopath."

"Maybe. But why stick a label on it? He's a successful producer. He's obsessed and he needs to be obsessed. Nothing really exists for him except the show. Not me, not you, not Donna. It may not be pretty, but there it is."

Jake draped a towel over his head and thought it over. "Okay, I get it. Sort of. Tell him I accept his apology. But I still think he's an insensitive dick."

Claire laughed. "I'll tell him. He won't care. But he won't forget either. When he doesn't need you anymore, look out. But another thing. We're not shooting tomorrow. Everybody's too upset."

"My, how human."

"Come on, don't judge us all by Quentin. I'm wondering if you might like to have lunch with me."

Caught off guard, Jake hesitated.

"Don't get all hot and bothered," she said. "It's just an innocent invitation for some seafood and a chat. I'm surrounded by kids here, chronological and emotional. I get a little starved for grown-up company. Can we say Louie's Backyard, one o'clock?"

At another fancy marina, this one at the north end of Key Largo, another fancy speedboat was being carefully tied into its berth. This craft was a sort of mica black flecked with metallic glints of forest green and midnight blue. Its dark windshield, now washed clean of spray, was molded and raked back like that of an Indy car. Roped off like a captured beast, the swelling hull still seemed to be straining forward, itching to climb the water as though it were a mountainside.

A man stepped off the boat. There was nothing remotely thuggish about him and in fact he was a very handsome man who looked considerably younger than his sixty or so years. His face and neck were beautifully tanned, just slightly leathery but in a way that flattered his flinty eyes. He wore pleated khaki shorts that ended just above his well-toned knees and a tidy polo shirt with a prestigious logo on the chest. His leather-laced boat shoes were the classic brand, and his salt-and-pepper hair was neither too short nor too long. There was a certain archaic elegance in the style of it; it lay in perfect waves, each a finger's breadth from the next, the way that 1940s crooners used to wear their hair.

The man walked up the dock, said cordial hellos to fellow boaters who were oiling teak or polishing brass or fiddling with balky engines. These other people called him Johnny and seemed proud he'd noticed them, glad of his attention. He continued on through the marina gate and toward a waterside restaurant called Handsome Johnny's Crab Joint. It was the tail end of lunchtime but the terrace tables were still full. He looked with an uneasy mix of satisfaction and contempt at the tourists in their lobster bibs, clumsily wielding picks and crackers, then he smoothly slipped into his purported place of business and disappeared from sight.

14

Joey Goldman had grown up in a tenement in Queens. His wife, Sandra Dugan, had lived in a fourth-floor walk-up in Brooklyn. Their home in Key West was therefore the fulfillment of a fantasy held by cramped apartment dwellers everywhere. It was mostly open space and windows. Glass doors slid aside to welcome in a safe and mild world. Skylights tracked the weather and the progress of the sun and moon. You stepped into that house and you felt sheltered but not trapped. There were plenty of ways to get out again.

Their backyard felt bigger than it really was. The shimmer from the pool somehow seemed to stretch the space above it. Patches of color—soft blue skyflower, flame red nicotiana—coaxed the eye from place to place. Small groupings of furniture created a cozy array of places to sit.

In one of those groupings, poolside, an old man was reclining with a chihuahua on his lap. The man had white hair, still quite thick, tinged with yellow at the upturning edges. He had black eyes set well back in their sockets and an enormous but stately nose that shaded one side of his face as if it were a sundial. He wore a resplendent linen shirt, lavender with navy piping on the placket and around the pockets; the same color had been used for his monogram, B d'A, done in fancy script. His long bony fingers encircled the little dog, sometimes petting it, other times just holding on.

He was scratching it behind the ears when Joey, who'd sprung up to answer the doorbell, came back into the yard with a fresh bottle of Chianti in his hand and their other dinner guest at his side. "Bert," he said, "meet Jake Benson. Jake, meet my oldest friend down here, Bert d'Ambrosia. First guy I met. Then it turned out he knew my father, my mother, my whole family from New York. Small world, right?"

Bert extended a veiny hand and said, "'Scuse me if I don't get up. Takes a while. Plus I got the stupid dog. This here's Don Giovanni. Say hello, Giovanni."

The dog allowed the old man to lift and wave its tiny paw. Then it licked the flat and reddish place where once upon a time its balls had been.

Joey sat, poured wine all around, and said to Jake, "I was just telling Bert about this craziness with Donna and the boat. Wanted to see what he made of it."

Bert ate an olive then dabbed his full lips on a napkin. "What's to make? It's a big fuckin' ocean out there. You got one broad swimmin' innee the ocean. You got one boat ridin' onnee ocean. They end up in the exact same spot at the exact same time. Coincidence?"

"It's a stretch," said Joey. "But it's tough to see—"

"What? A motive? Crazy fuckin' world, who needs a motive anymore? People feel like runnin' someone over, they do it. Wha'd you say this girl's last name is?"

"Alvarez."

"From Miami, right? Cuban probably. They got their issues. The Castro bullshit. The smuggling bullshit." To Jake he said, "You know this Donna person?"

"Just met last night. Strange circumstance. I was drunk. She was naked."

"Match made in heaven," the old man said.

"Nothing happened. We talked."

Bert sipped some wine, then, as was becoming an ever more frequent occurrence, his mind skipped back to what he'd been saying before. "Yeah, the Cubans, they have their little wars, their little squabbles with certain people I used to know. Plus, from what you said about the boat–Cigarette or something close, right?"

"Big, fast, and dark," Jake put in.

"Ya see, that tells me something. That's not a boat that citizens take for a spin on a weekday morning. That's a working boat, if you catch my drift." He'd put his hands back on the dog. Now he turned his big face down and spoke to it. "You and me, we've took some rides on boats like that, ain't we, Giovanni."

The dog flicked out a quick pink tongue and kissed the old man on the tip of his giant nose.

Jake drank some wine and hid behind his glass a moment. He needed some time to gather his thoughts. He knew it was improbable, ridiculous, but he couldn't help thinking that Joey's best friend Bert looked more than a little bit like an old Mafioso. He talked more than a little bit like an old Mafioso. And he brought out more of an Outer Borough accent in Joey than Jake had noticed before; a hint of social club accent almost. Then again, Jake's imagination tended to run away with him; professional hazard, after all. But he couldn't help mulling the possibility, and Bert d'Ambrosia somehow seemed to sense him mulling it. When Jake lowered the wineglass from his face, the two men shared a fleeting but entirely candid glance.

Jake's eyes asked: Are you?

Bert's twinkling gaze and merest hint of a sly smile said: Yeah, what of it?

Jake briefly wondered why he wasn't more uneasy or surprised, why this latest wrinkle simply struck him as one more thing that might happen in Key West. Was it just the heat? The haze of humidity that blurred sharp edges and usual assumptions? He held Bert's stare a heartbeat longer, until Sandra appeared in the open doorway and called over to Joey. "Can you give me a hand in here? I'm cooking on four burners."

Inside the airy kitchen, water was heating for pasta. Spinach was sautéing. Garlic was slowly toasting and tomatoes were cooking down, farting out a viscous bubble now and then. Joey picked up a wooden spoon and started stirring.

"How's Bert tonight?" asked Sandra, brushing back a wisp of caramel-colored hair from her forehead. Just past forty, Sandra didn't look her age and never had. Twenty years in the Keys and her skin was still smooth and unfreckled.

Just slightly defensively, Joey said, "He's fine. Sharp as a tack."

"He still calling the dog by the wrong name?"

"Sandra, what does it matter what he calls the dog?"

"It worries me, that's all."

It worried Joey too but he fought against admitting it. "You think the dog cares what he calls it? Six months ago dog was on death row, one bowl of kibble from the gas chamber. He's happy to be called anything. Plus he had a stupid name before. Nacho. That's like, whaddyacallit, racial profiling. Mexican dog, name him after an appetizer. That's not right."

Sandra said, "I'm not talking about the dog's ethnic background, okay? I'm talking about Bert. I sometimes worry he's not so with it anymore. That he's living in the past."

Reluctantly, Joey said, "On this one thing, maybe. Other than that, he's sharp, he's fine."

Sandra said nothing. Joey stirred tomatoes. Agitated, he stirred them a little too hard so that hot red starbursts shot over the edges of the pan. After a moment he went on, "Come on, Sandra, guy's almost ninety, he's entitled to a little…a little, let's call it eccentricity."

His wife just leaned over and kissed him softly on the cheek.

15

"We need something sexy," the publicist was saying. Her name was Jacqueline Mayfield. She was six-foot-one, African American, and well on her way to becoming legendary for her persuasiveness. Her secret for getting the media to do her bidding was that she didn't just convey a message, she became the message. She put her whole self into it, and everything about her whole self was commanding and large. Big shoulders, big hips, big voice, big smile, big scowl, big laugh. "A random, non-fatal accident just isn't sexy," she went on. "An injury to a stuntwoman just isn't sexy."

"Inconveniently, though," Claire Segal say dryly, "an accidental injury to a stuntwoman is what happened."

"Maybe," said Jacqueline. "But come on. We all know there's a difference between what happened and what the story is."

They were meeting in Jacqueline's suite at The Nest, the discreet and elegant boutique hotel where the more important people from *Adrift* were housed. Rob Stanton, the director, was at the meeting, along with a couple of key cast members. Quentin Dole and several suits from the network were video-conferenced in from Los Angeles; their slightly distorted faces swam and smeared across computer screens; they looked like fish bumping their noses against the glass of an aquarium.

One of the suits, his words just slightly lagging the blurry movement of his lips, said, "I think what's right in front of us is pretty damn good. Classic human interest. The stuntwoman—what's her name again?—she's a perfect unsung hero."

Jacqueline was shaking her big impressive head. "Hold that thought. *Unsung.* The little people behind the stars. That's old. That's a one-day story. We can do better than that."

"We better do better than that," said another of the suits. He leaned forward as he said it so that his swooping face looked both menacing and entirely goofy. "Look, the show's losing momentum. Ratings have been flat the last three weeks."

"Flat at a damn high level," put in another executive.

"Flat is flat," came the reply. "And flat today is down tomorrow. We don't a need a cuddly little human interest segment, we need some real heat."

The first suit still liked his own idea. "Can we get a crew into the hospital? That'd be great! You see this woman, the I.V. stuff, maybe in traction, some bandages on her head, you realize, *Wow, people risk their lives to make this show…* "

"What people?" said Jacqueline. "Who's risking their life? That's what we need to be asking. If it's just some acrobat that no one's ever heard of who gets dinged up on the job, that's not much of a story."

"She's not an acrobat," said Claire. "She's a good actress who does stunts. And she's not *dinged up.* She almost died."

"But she didn't," said the publicist. "Amen. So can we please get back to what we're doing here?"

There was a somewhat frosty pause.

Finally, Quentin Dole spoke up. His lean face looked very bony on the computer screen and his glasses were halfway between light and dark, somewhat iridescent. He said, "I like what I'm hearing from Jacqueline, but please let's back up a step. Let's think about some context. Not so much what happened, but how it happened, why it happened. What was Donna doing when the accident occurred?"

No one wanted to risk a wrong answer and for a moment no one spoke. Then one of the suits ventured, "Swimming?"

"Very good," said Quentin wiltingly. "That would be the activity most often associated with getting run over by a boat. But I don't think that's the part that matters here. What matters is the role she was playing. She was doubling for Candace."

Claire said, "Now wait a second—"

Quentin didn't. "She was dressed like Candace. She had the wig on. She was continuing a scene that Candace had started—"

"Bingo," said Jacqueline. "There's our story."

"Bullshit," said Claire. "That's not our story. It's nonsense. It's a lie. It's irresponsible."

"I like it," said one of the suits.

"It isn't irresponsible," Quentin said. "It's just spin. Jacqueline's right. What's more interesting? A stunt girl has an accident, or maybe it wasn't an accident and the victim was supposed to be our star?"

"That's the way to go," said Jacqueline. "Definitely. It'll be the lead on all the daytime programs, all the magazines."

"Quentin," said Claire, "you can't do this. This is not the fucking show. This is real. Someone got hurt."

Ignoring her, one of the suits said, "We just have to keep it a *what if* kind of thing. Nothing too specific. Otherwise we'll never get it past Legal."

"Yeah, perfect," said Jacqueline. "Just raise the possibility. Plant a seed. Leave it open-ended. Same way the show leaves things open-ended. Get that echo going."

Claire said, "This is sick."

One of the suits said, "This is great. The whole country'll be talking about it. People who've never even seen the show will be talking about it."

Rob Stanton said, "Wait a second. Aren't we forgetting something? Someone's feelings?"

The notion seemed to usher in a moment of abashed silence. People dropped each other's eyes like hot pans. Then the director went on.

"You okay with this, Candace? Concocting this rumor that maybe someone's trying to kill you?"

The star didn't answer right away but chose to milk the scene. She pursed then licked her sensuous lips. She blinked her violet eyes and let them drift out of focus into some dreamy middle distance. She began to speak then stopped, as if the words were costing her too much. Finally, in a voice barely above a whisper, she said, "Someone is."

For a moment no one breathed. The publicist silently put down the pen she'd been holding. The smeared faces on the computer screens were studies in bewilderment.

Then, with a hack of a laugh, one of the suits said, "Isn't she terrific? Look at that, she's on board in a heartbeat. She could sell that story to anyone."

Uneasily, people swayed toward joining in the laugh but didn't get quite as far as laughing.

Without raising her eyes, Candace said, "It isn't just a story. I think someone's trying to kill me."

The suit who'd been laughing went silent with the others. Quentin Dole and Jacqueline Mayfield looked past each other like people lost in a cave.

Then Candace laughed. The laugh was cloaked in geniality but it was a mocking laugh, a reveling in her skill at fakery, her capacity to fool. Throwing back her rich black hair, she said, "Had you going, didn't I?"

Everyone except Claire Segal pretended to find this rather funny.

16

At yet another fancy marina, this one right there in Key West, mere blocks from downtown, a third speedboat was being berthed, this time under the last mauve glow of dusk. In the soft and shifting light, the boat's exact color was impossible to discern. Midnight blue? Deep-space purple? Obsidian black? Huge twin engines freighted the stern and lifted the bulbous hull so that the boat had rather the posture of a crouching lion, the hindquarters held low, coiled to spring, the chest and shoulders tensed to strike.

When the last line had been cleated off, a dockhand laid a gangway across the transom. A woman in large amber sunglasses stepped off the speedboat. She was tall, lean, and blonde, her hair becomingly wild and spiky from the sea breeze and the spray. She wore tight pink pants that buttoned off just below the knee; on her feet were gladiatorial-looking sandals with mid-height heels and straps that climbed and wrapped around her calves like strangler vines. Over a bikini top that was little more than strings and patches, she wore a light black leather jacket that was far too snug to zip; it left a slice of her exposed from below the navel to her taut and suntanned throat.

Swinging a stylish bag that seemed able to contain not much more than some make-up and a change of clothes, she sashayed down the dock, the heels of her sandals clicking softly as she headed for her hotel, The Nest, where she had a reservation under a name that was not her own.

Back in Joey and Sandra's backyard, dinner was well advanced. Much wine had been drunk and more was on the table; the yellow glow of hurricane lamps reflected off the glasses. The companionable smells of garlic and olive oil were mingling with the salt air and the jasmine. Expertly twirling pasta while also fondling the chihuahua in his lap, Bert said to Jake, "So Joey tells me you're a writer. Whaddya write?"

Jake sipped some wine and blithely said, "Whatever I can get a contract for."

"Ah, you work on contract. Me and Joey, we know some guys who work on contract, don't we, Joey?"

"Don't even go there, Bert."

"Hey, just messin' around."

Hoping to steer the conversation elsewhere, Sandra said, "You know what I think must be great about being a writer? The mental health part."

"There's a mental health part?" said Jake.

"I mean, people hold so much inside. What they're afraid of. Who they're mad at. What they think is all screwed up about the world. Writers have a way to get all that off their chests. Don't they?"

Jake considered as he put some salad on his plate. "Sometimes. Sort of. Maybe."

Bert said, "What are you, a politician?"

"It's just that it's complicated. You know, people think writers just sit down and let it all hang out, tell the world what they really think, write whatever they feel like writing. But if you're on a job—"

"Y'ever write your own stuff?" Bert cut in. He hadn't meant to interrupt, or not that sharply at least. But that was one of the things about being old: If you wanted to ask a question it paid to ask it quickly, before it slipped your mind. "Ya know," he went on, "just stuff ya wanna say?"

Jake seemed caught up short. He drank some wine then said almost apologetically, "I used to."

"Used to?" Joey said.

Jake gave a little laugh. "Hey, no one dreams of being a ghostwriter when he grows up. I wrote my own stuff. Sure I did. Just didn't quite work out."

He briefly looked down. His eyes landed on the chihuahua, which had lifted its nose onto the table and was sniffing at Bert's plate.

"How come?" the old man asked.

"Oh boy," said Jake. "I haven't talked about this in a lot of years."

He nudged his glass in Joey's direction. Joey filled it for him.

"I think the problem was that I cared too much. I wanted every word to be perfect. I tried so hard to make it perfect that it probably wasn't very good. At least that's what a few people told me."

"Who?" said Sandra. "What people?"

"A few editors and agents."

"Fuck do they know?" Bert said. "'Scuse my language, Sandra."

Jake made a sound somewhere between a dry laugh and a snort. "Fair question."

Sandra, trying to be helpful, said, "Well, it all seems to have turned out for the best."

Jake didn't quite know what to say to that. He tossed her a smile that was meant as thanks but felt uncomfortable at the edges of his mouth.

Sandra, not quite comfortable herself, went on. "I mean, you seem to have a nice career. You get interesting work—"

"Which way felt better?" Bert put in, once again a little off the beat, unintentionally abrupt, blurting out a fleeting thought before it vanished.

"Excuse me?"

"Which was more fun? I mean, getting paid is good, money's good, I'm not knockin' money, plus it's none of my business and all of that, but I'm sittin' here, I'm listenin', and I can't help wondering, just wondering ya know, if maybe you were better off before. Happier, I mean. But hey, sorry, none of my business. I'll shut up now. Sorry."

Jake picked up his wineglass, put it down again. Crickets rasped. Tree toads made their miniature bleating sounds.

After a long moment, Sandra said. "Well. Anybody ready for dessert?

17

"You like Negronis?" Claire asked.

"Don't know. Never had one."

"But you like martinis."

"That would be a yes."

"Then have a Negroni. Gin, Campari, a little vermouth. It's like a killer martini in a pink tutu."

"Sounds a little strong for lunch."

"Oh, it is, believe me. And I almost never drink at lunch."

"Then why—"

"Because I'm furious."

They were sitting on the oceanfront deck at Louie's Backyard. It seemed a hard day to stay mad. A cool breeze was perfectly balancing the heat of the sun. Ripples that now and then spilled over into tiny whitecaps were chasing each other across the surface of the sea. Green-tinged clouds hung near the horizon, never coming any closer.

Jake asked what she was furious about.

"We'll get to that. How are you?"

It was seemingly the simplest of questions, generally calling for a scripted one-word reply, but in that moment Jake found it a stupefying riddle that he didn't want to try to answer all at once. He said, "We'll get to that too. After the Negronis."

Waiting for the drinks, they looked out at the twinkling water and, somewhat shyly, at each other. Claire was wearing a blue sundress that tied behind her neck. Her bare arms were toned but slender; there was a pretty arc where her neck flowed down to her collarbones.

Jake said, "You look different today."

She flushed just slightly at the comment. "Get to wear my play clothes. And I'm not carrying the goddamn clipboard."

"Your hair looks different too," he ventured. It was softer today, freer. Wisps of it were lifted by the breeze and waved against her cheek.

She flushed a tiny bit more but said, "We aren't on a date. Agreed?"

To Jake this didn't exactly sound like scolding and it didn't exactly sound like teasing, though it did sound just a little bit like both. He said, "Agreed. Just making an observation."

The drinks arrived. They looked benign enough. Healthy even, with a coiling twist of orange peel. They clinked glasses and after the first sip Jake said, "So, you want to tell me why you're furious?"

Claire looked at the ocean, took another sip and said, "It's just the stupid show. This big successful cash cow of a program. I just don't like what it does to people."

She told him about the meeting with the publicist and the suits.

"Not a shred of real concern for Donna," she said. "Not even a shred of curiosity about what really happened. All they care about is buzz. Spinning a tidy little story for the media. And the sick part? It'll work. It'll work brilliantly."

She paused just long enough to nip at her drink, then went on. "The publicist has been talking it up all night, all morning. She's already got segments lined up on *ET* and *Inside Hollywood*. *People* and *Us* have committed to stories. Candace is in her glory, of course. The diva in danger. The star as target. Like real life has become one big outtake from the show. The whole thing's disgusting. Aren't you glad you asked?"

Before Jake could answer, a waiter appeared to take their order. Claire said she was too mad to eat much, maybe just some oysters. Jake asked for the same. Then he said, "Actually, I am glad I asked. I'm ticked off about some of this same stuff."

Claire heard herself say, "Even though Donna is not your girl-friend?" She hoped it would come out as a little joke, but it didn't really sound that way because today she truly wanted to settle the question.

"She's not. Never was. This isn't even about Donna. Not really."

"So it's about–?"

Jake struggled to explain. He was surprised how difficult it was. He described things, explained things, for a living. It was harder when the thing he was explaining was gnawing at his guts. "Yesterday," he began, "when Quentin called—"

"And you hung up on him," Claire put in.

"Right. You know, for such a smart guy, his timing was incredibly dumb. I'm upset about what happened, it's horribly fresh in my mind, and he picks that moment to pitch me on this preposterous fake story about the earth cracking open. And the two things side by side made my job seem so ridiculous, so trivial, so embarrassing that writing this cynical hack bullshit is what I'm doing with my life—"

He broke off because Claire had put her hand on his. This was so unexpected that it sent a spasm all up his arm. Her hand was cool from cradling her glass. She let it rest on his for just a moment then pulled it back. He kept feeling it after it was gone. She said, "You're being awfully tough on yourself."

He shook his head. "No, not tough enough. I take the easy road. I have for years and years. Last night, I was having dinner with this old Mafia guy—"

That's when the waiter appeared with the oysters. His eyes widened just slightly and he set the plates down very carefully. Before he could slip away Claire asked him for another round of drinks.

"Mafia guy?" she said to Jake.

"Long story."

"I've got time."

So he told her about his evening at Joey's.

"This old guy Bert," he said, "who's either like a Mob Zen master or totally out of it or probably both, starts asking me all this stuff I haven't thought about in years. Why'd I stop writing what I wanted to? Which way was I happier? And I swear, by the end of the dinner I felt like I'd been turned completely inside out."

The fresh drinks arrived. For a moment Jake just stared at his.

Claire said, "Tough day all around. But I like talking with you. I sometimes forget what it sounds like when people actually say what they mean."

He looked up and met her eyes. They were the same color as the sea behind her.

They started in on the oysters, salty with brine and sizzling with the tang of Key lime. They sucked them straight from the shells. The shells left an astringent, stony dryness on their tongues and lips; the dryness in turn was bathed away by the clean burn of gin.

At some point Jake said, "And another thing about these people I had dinner with. They don't for a second believe what happened to Donna was an accident."

The abrupt segue caught Claire by surprise. She paused with an oyster partway to her lips.

"They've seen too many bad things done with speedboats. They don't know who and they don't why but they're sure someone did this on purpose."

Claire put the oyster back on her plate.

"And here's the part that's making me nuts," Jake went on. "There's this real story right in front of us. Real people. Real blood. Real justice to be done. Or not. And everybody's too wrapped up in their own bullshit to pay any attention to it. The cops don't seem to care. Your people from the show don't want any nasty truth to get in the way of their fairy tale. And me, I'm no better. I was there, I saw it happen, and now I'm supposed to step calmly away, forget all about it, and write an idiotic piece of trash about nothing whatsoever."

He broke off and reached for his drink. Claire used her tiny fork to push at the melting ice beneath her oysters. Then she said, "But you don't want to step away."

"I really don't know what I want."

Claire blinked off toward the ocean. Weighing her words, she said, "I think maybe you do."

He looked at her, not exactly asking for help but opening himself to accept it.

"I think you want your own book."

He licked his lips. He found nothing to say.

"A real book," she went on, "with a real story. A story that won't just come to you, that you'll have to go out and find."

He looked away a moment and drummed his fingertips lightly on the table. When he brought his eyes back to Claire, his gaze had narrowed and firmed and she couldn't quite tell if this was from staring at the glinting water or from something like resolve.

Softly, carefully, she said, "I have an idea. How about we finish our drinks, hop a cab, and see if we can visit Donna?"

18

At Florida Keys General if not on national TV, Donna Alvarez was already an established star.

She'd amazed the doctors with her resilience, her vigor and her will. Mere hours after sustaining her gruesome injuries, she'd been moved out of the ICU, unhooked from the now unneeded monitors that tracked her rock-solid vital signs. By the next morning, she'd been half-propped up in bed and was sipping lukewarm broth through a straw. By afternoon, weaned down to a modest regimen of Vicodin, she was more or less alert and chatting with the nurses. Not that she didn't bear evidence of what she'd been through. On her right side, a bulge in her pale green hospital gown traced out the place where a wound was heavily bandaged over a zigzag pattern of stitches. Her right arm was lifted at an awkward angle, the dislocated shoulder immobilized by a kind of heavy-duty bubble wrap, the hand taped to a trapeze on a frame.

When Claire and Jake, bearing flowers and chocolates, were shown into her room, her eyes, just slightly veiled with the merciful haze of painkillers, were riveted to a gossip show on television.

Candace McBride was on the screen, talking earnestly about "the near-tragedy on the set of *Adrift*." Asked if she thought the guilty speedboat might in fact have been stalking her, the diva put a tremble in her lower lip and looked away. Asked if she had enemies, she was all bewilderment and hurt feelings. "I get along with people. I love people. But fans of the show are so passionate, so involved. Maybe they don't realize where the character ends and the real me begins."

With her good hand Donna switched off the set. Before she even said hello to her visitors, she said in a voice slightly thickened by her meds, "Can you believe it? I'm lying here with my arm stuck out like I'm saluting Hitler, my side feels like a half-chewed burger, and that cunt still thinks it's all about her."

Claire said, "Donna, Donna, so glad to see they haven't broken your spirit."

"They've broken every other fucking thing." Then, to Jake, she said, "Hello, handsome. Thanks for the lift." Her slightly blurry eyes flicking back to Claire, she went on. "How's the shooting going? Hope I haven't messed up the schedule."

"Actually, you have. Big time. No one's working today. Everybody's too upset."

"Upset. Why? Because maybe it was supposed to be Candace lying here?"

"No. Upset about you. Everyone was really worried."

At this expression of some basic kindness, Donna's bravado finally let go. Her face softened, she squirmed in bed and couldn't quite suppress a wince of pain from her wound. Quietly she said, "It's really nice you came to see me." Her gaze drifted toward the fancily wrapped box that Jake was holding in his hand. "Looks like chocolates. What kind?"

Jake had no idea. He'd rushed into a shop and grabbed some. "Um, assorted."

"Expensive?"

"Very."

"Good. I like expensive chocolates. It's really nice you came to see me. Did I say that already?"

Claire and Jake shared a quick glance. Claire said, "You must be tired. We'll come back another time soon."

"No!" said Donna. There was a hint of pleading in it. "Stay. I'm fine. Just a little groggy. My energy sort of comes and goes. It's so nice that you came. Sit down. Sit down."

They pulled over squeaky metal chairs and sat down at the bedside. The smells of the hospital wafted over them—plasma, disinfectant, overcooked vegetables on lunch trays.

Donna gestured weakly toward the blank TV. "This bullshit with Candace. Is that what people really think?"

Claire said, "People, like, the public? Who knows what they think? It's just something Quentin and the publicist cooked up for the media."

Donna gave as much of a one-sided shrug as she could manage. "Figured it was something like that. Makes sense. Better story."

"Are you sure of that?" Jake asked.

Donna's fragile focus seemed to wander. "Sure of what?"

"That the made-up version is a better story. Maybe what really happened is a better story."

Donna said nothing.

Jake went on. "What do you think really happened?"

Donna came close to a small, hoarse laugh. "I think I got run over by a fucking boat."

"Just like that? By accident?"

The stuntwoman let her eyes fall closed. She kept them shut for long enough that her visitors had time to wonder if she had drifted off to sleep. Then she opened them again and said, "I hope so. I hope it was an accident."

"But you're not sure," Jake pressed.

She turned her head and shifted her legs beneath the sheet, trying to wriggle up taller in the bed. The effort cost her pain. Through a grimace she said, "How could I be sure?"

She zoned out for another few seconds then licked her dry lips and added very softly, "Someone took my script."

"Your script?" said Claire.

Donna, fighting against a humiliating fatigue, kept squirming, trying to sit up higher, "I couldn't find it that morning. Yesterday morning. I looked everywhere."

Claire said gently, "It'll turn up."

"No it won't," said Donna with a kind of muted certainty. "I've never lost a script. I never would. Someone took it." She tried to pivot onto her good elbow and flinched. "Why would someone take my script?"

A nurse walked into the room just then. He found his star patient half-leaning out of bed, clearly drained and agitated. He quickly moved over to soothe her then politely but firmly he shooed the visitors away.

When Jake and Claire were nearly out the door, Donna managed to lean over to see beyond the nurse's body. "Come back tomorrow. Please. I'll be all better by tomorrow."

Jake promised that he would.

Donna said, "Bring more chocolates."

19

Back at the compound, Jake walked around the pool and beyond the pumps and filters to the shed where Bryce lived. He found the door wide open, sagging on corroded hinges. The slender young man in the red sarong was lying on his bed, staring at the ceiling.

"Hi, Bryce. Got a minute?"

"No. I'm busy."

"Oh."

"Just kidding. What's up?" He came to a half-recumbent position, leaning on his elbows.

"Got a question for you. The other day, when Donna's old boyfriend—"

"Ace, his name is."

"Okay, when Ace was here. Tell me more about what happened."

"Why?"

"I'm just interested, that's all."

"Why you want to know? You playing detective or something?"

Jake said nothing.

"Might be kind of cool if you decided to play detective."

Jake stayed quiet and after a moment Bryce went on.

"Isn't much to tell. He barged into the compound, headed to Donna's place. I told him he shouldn't go in. He went in anyway."

"He had a key?"

"He said he did. I think he was bluffing. Donna had the lock changed when she threw him out. He sort of blocked the view with his body. Took him a little longer to open the door than it would have with a key. Not much longer. Everyone has shitty locks down here."

"And he took something, right? I heard you say he was taking something that wasn't his."

"Yeah, a notebook. That old three-ring kind, like in school."

"Her script?"

Bryce shrugged, his thin shoulders reaching almost to his earlobes. "I guess. I used to see her sitting with that notebook, sort of mouthing her lines."

Jake said, "She has no lines. She just does stunts."

"Mouthing other people's lines, then. You know, pretending like she was a star, I guess."

The observation depressed Jake. He looked down at his feet then at the wall behind Bryce's bed. That's when he noticed that the wall was totally plastered in carefully tacked up pages from illustrated calendars. The pages seemed at first to suggest a preoccupation, maybe even an obsession, with the clipped and steady drumbeat of time. But then he realized that the months were hung in no particular order and had been lifted out of different years. This splatter of chronology, more in keeping with a long dream than with waking life, intrigued him. Was it a sort of uncaptioned scrapbook of special moments or did Bryce just like the peculiar array of photographs—the Eiffel Tower, Whitney Houston, baby kangaroos—that were appended to the random months?

After a silence, he said, "What's with the calendars?"

"What about them?"

"They're not in any order."

Bryce quietly disagreed. "They're in an order. Just not the usual one."

He said this with such serene finality that Jake thought it would be rude to press the matter further. He thanked Bryce for his time and turned to go.

To his back Bryce said, "Hey, I have a kind of cool idea. If you're really going to play detective, maybe I could be your helper. Any chance?"

Poolside at The Nest, a tall, lean blonde in amber sunglasses and a yellow thong bikini was stashing her gladiator sandals beneath her lounge and preparing to rub suntan lotion on her feet and legs. This rubbing turned out to be a slow and languorous process; in fact it bordered on the lewd. She caressed her insteps then massaged each facet of her shapely ankles. Her calves she anointed with long firm strokes that traced out filaments of muscle and painted a moist lubricated sheen onto her skin. She cupped her knees to baste them, then pampered her thighs, inside and out, high up toward her loins, the taut flesh quivering just slightly as her hands passed slowly over. She twisted on her hips, oiling first one buttock then the other, giving the merest suggestion of a brisk spank along with the caress.

There was one thing that was very clear about this little ritual. It wasn't just about sun protection. The woman wanted to be looked at. And she was. Straight men looked at her with barely disguised Pavlovian appetite. Gay men studied and admired the bitch-goddess aloofness. Women looked at the bold display with silent disapproval, mingled, perhaps, with just a touch of secret envy of her brazen confidence.

But if the woman wanted to be looked at, she didn't quite want to be seen. She returned none of the glances thrown her way. She lay back on her lounge, picked up a magazine, and largely disappeared behind it, her eyes emerging only briefly when some new person appeared at the edges of her vision. Furtively, she glanced at each new passerby but lost interest in less than a heartbeat.

She was still lying there when Claire returned from the hospital and was walking through the pool area to her room. The woman peeked quickly over the top of her magazine and was already lowering it again when Claire said a brief but friendly hello. The woman lifted her face just long enough to answer in kind and in that moment Claire thought she looked somehow familiar. "Do I know you?" she asked.

"No. I'm sure you don't."

The denial required only an instant of shared gaze, but in that tiny interval Claire's impression deepened. She couldn't quite put her finger on why. It wasn't the surface details of the face, exactly; more to do with the structure of it—the placement of the eyes, the slope of the jawline, the angle of the ears. "From Los Angeles, maybe?"

"No. I'm sorry. Never been there."

"My mistake," said Claire with an apologetic little smile.

The woman didn't answer and didn't smile back, simply raised the magazine again to shade her face and shoulders while her legs gleamed like washed bronze in the sunshine.

20

In his spacious office that was well insulated against the heat and tumult of the kitchen, surrounded by signed photos of celebrities who'd eaten in his restaurant, Handsome Johnny Burke was talking on his cell phone. His feet were up on his desk and he leaned far back in a chair that could swivel every which way. His voice was animated, his gestures were expansive. He asked lots of questions, as though he was catching up with a long lost friend. "So it's going well?" he said avidly. "Going like you hoped it would?"

"Even better," said the voice at the other end of the line. "Three hundred thousand hits on the website, today alone. The publicist is on a tear. Everybody's talking."

"And the actress? She's doing her part?"

"Shamelessly."

"Shameless in Hollywood is good," said Handsome Johnny. "Even I learned that. And I didn't learn too damn much."

In this Johnny was being modest. When, some forty-something years before, he'd moved from Baltimore to Los Angeles with nothing but his good looks and his vague but fierce ambition to break into the movies, he'd learned plenty. He'd learned, for instance, that it wasn't only starlets who paid their dues on the casting couch. It was the '70s; things were weird, many varieties of sex and drugs around, and Johnny Burke did what he thought he needed to do. The payback, though, never seemed to be a role, only an audition that didn't quite pan out, a screen test that didn't go so well. Broke, lacking prospects, he soon figured out that supplying drugs was a better deal than using them himself. This, in turn, led him downward toward the stratum of small-time punks and wannabe gangsters who loitered at the edges of the entertainment business, stealing cars occasionally, running contraband from Tijuana. At moments Johnny Burke blamed Hollywood for turning him bad; at other moments he perversely reveled in the acknowledgment that he'd always been a lousy person just waiting to happen. Still, it had genuinely surprised him to realize he'd become a criminal.

Now the voice at the other end of the phone pinched down into an uncomfortable laugh and said, "You learned enough to get out."

Something in the simple words seemed to sting Johnny Burke. His shoulders sagged, his voice lost some of its ebullience. "Yeah, I did. With plenty of regrets. I did."

But what did he have to regret? His ambition to be an actor had been mocked and tarnished beyond recognition; nothing left to mourn on that score. There was certainly no nostalgia in moving on from his dirtbag Los Angeles companions. The only thing worth regretting was that a few months before he bolted town, Johnny had gotten someone pregnant. She was a casual girlfriend, no great love, but she was determined to have the baby. To Johnny this was utterly unthinkable. His attitude was not entirely selfish. He didn't want to subject a child to a father like him in a world like the one he knew. He denied paternity and headed to Florida.

"We don't need to talk about regrets," the phone voice said. "We've been all through that."

"I still feel it, Quentin. What can I say?"

"You don't need to say anything, Dad."

Handsome Johnny pulled his feet down from the desk, rocked forward in his chair, and leaned on his elbows, one hand raking through the waves in his hair. "It must be hard for you to say that word."

"It is. The truth? I say it, it's like I'm choking on a piece of steak. And in another way it feels good. All fucked up, I guess."

"I'm sorry, Quentin."

"Stop that. It's all fine now. For both of us."

Johnny gave a secret wince at that. Things with him were fine only if you didn't look too closely. He owned a restaurant. Through his old West Coat connections he helped to finance movies. Lately he'd even been tracked down and reached out to by the highly successful son he'd given up on ever knowing. It might have passed for a happy ending to a sordid story but none of it was what it seemed. The restaurant was his in name alone; in fact it was a money laundering machine for a Miami mobster. The movie financing also came from dirty money and was little more than loan-sharking by a more prestigious name.

And this sudden contact with the son, this parody of family—if it was the sweetest thing in Johnny's life, it was also in some way the creepiest. As a father he'd been a runaway and a deadbeat. What could he offer his grown son now except a tardy and rather mawkish love marbled with a guilt that did no one any good? And why should the son feel anything other than rage and loathing toward the parent who'd bolted on him? In their conversations he pretended to something almost like natural affection, but below the surface of their cordiality there was blaming, and also a kind of horrid symmetry. Handsome Johnny, knowing all the while that nothing could make up for his long ago abandonment, would do anything for Quentin. Quentin, without a qualm and in fact with a certain vengeful relish, would ask anything of Johnny. Their relationship was a conspiracy of futile amends and futile getting even.

Trying to rally from his suddenly dark mood, Johnny Burke said, "I'm pulling for you, kid. I'll do anything to make it up. You know that, right?"

"I do," said Quentin Dole.

"Okay. Call me when the ratings come in. The second you see the numbers. Call me. Okay?"

The producer of *Adrift* promised that he would.

21

"Feeling better?"

"Depends. You bring more chocolates?"

"You ate the other ones already?"

"Some I ate, some I gave to people. People are nice here. Treat me like I matter. I could almost get used to it."

Producing a package from behind his back, Jake said, "Then it's a good thing I brought a bigger box today."

Donna squirmed against her pillows, managed to lean forward for a closer look. She no longer winced every time she moved, though the trapeze from which her arm was still suspended squeaked like a hamster wheel from even the smallest motion.

"Your eyes look much better," Jake said. "Still on pain pills?"

"Stopped 'em this morning. Waste of good drugs. Plus I don't like feeling dopey. Where's Claire? Back to shooting?"

Jake acknowledged that she was.

"Well," said Donna, "the show must go on and all that happy horseshit. Let's see those chocolates."

He handed her the box. With her one good hand she joyfully but ineffectively clawed at the ribbon and the foil. "Fuck. I can't get it open. Help me."

He leaned in close, smelled the austere hospital soap with which she'd been bathed. She looked at the extravagant chocolates and said, "Wow. Are you trying to get me into bed?"

Jake said, "You're in bed already."

"Okay, okay. So you don't want to answer the question." She picked up a truffle and bit into it. "I guess Claire's more your type anyway."

"Let's not even go there."

"She's smart. Successful. Classy."

"All true. And she's a colleague. That's all."

"*Colleague*," Donna mimicked, giving it a very hoity-toity sound. "I love that word. So respectable. So serious. Like you can't fuck someone because she's a colleague?"

Jake laughed. "You do have a gift for the profane."

Donna rolled right along. "Now, I wouldn't know. About *colleagues*, I mean. I don't have *colleagues*, just knuckleheads I work with. But I've heard rumors that people poke their colleagues all the time."

Jake popped another *bonbon* into her mouth to get her off the subject. Then he pulled over a chair and sat down at the bedside. "Donna, listen, there's something I want to talk with you about."

She heard the change in his tone, seemed to have anticipated it, in fact, and wherever he was going she didn't want to follow. Lightly, she said, "Uh-oh."

Jake chose not to be deflected. "I know who took your script. And I'm guessing you know it too."

Donna settled back on her pillow and turned her face away. "I don't want to talk about that."

"Why not?"

She didn't answer.

Jake went on. "His name is Ace. He's your former boyfriend. You used to fight a lot and he'd make threats. I think he's from Miami."

Donna said, "You trying to play detective or something? How you know all that?"

"Doesn't matter how I know it. But what I'm wondering is why this guy would want your script."

"Who knows? Maybe he's auditioning. Everybody wants to be on TV, right?"

"Donna, please, I'm serious. Here's what I'm wondering. Maybe he wanted to know when they'd be shooting what. When you'd be in the water."

"That isn't in the script," she said. She was silent for a moment, then turned her head slightly away and added very softly, "It's in something called the one-line."

Jake arced an arm around her pillow, tried to coax her eyes back toward him. "And was the one-line also in your notebook?"

She didn't answer and she didn't let her head be turned.

Jake said, "So he knew the shooting schedule."

Grudgingly she said, "Lots of people know the schedule."

"But lots of people haven't threatened you," said Jake. "Have they?"

"Ace wouldn't do this to me," she said.

"Someone did."

"He doesn't have a speedboat."

"He could get one. Anybody could."

Donna was silent for a moment, looking at nothing. Then her eyes swept right past Jake toward the box of chocolates. She reached for one but he pulled the box away.

"Don't you want to know who did this to you? Don't you even care?"

"What's the difference who did it? It's done. It's over. Give me the fucking chocolates."

He held them out of reach. "Why are you protecting him?"

Donna fell back on the pillow and gave her head a shake. She threw Jake a look that was equal parts fondness and exasperation. "You're an idiot," she said. "A classic case of a brainy guy who's really, really clueless."

He absorbed the comment, said nothing.

Leaning forward as far as she could manage, she went on, "I'm not protecting him, you jerk. I'm protecting you."

He put the candy down where she could reach it. "Me?"

"Look, Jake, you're a nice person. You hang around with other nice people. *Colleagues.* There's a lot of stuff you just don't get. Ace, I tell myself he means well or at least meant well once upon a time, but the people he hangs with, works with, they steal cars, break knees, set things on fire. They're gangsters and bullies and that's what he seems to be becoming, too. You don't want to mess around with him."

Out of his depth, Jake said nothing.

Donna went on. "So why was I with him in the first place? That's what you're thinking, right? Well, I know what Dr. Phil would say: low self-esteem. Might be something to it. When I started in with Ace, what was I? High school dropout whose best subject was gymnastics. Dopey girl trying to take some acting classes. Who did I expect to be with, Barack Obama?"

She reached for a candy, pulled her hand back.

"But it wasn't only that. His group, his world, it excited me. For a while. I admit it. Champagne, hundred dollar bills. Plus I told myself the usual bullshit—he wasn't like the others, there was something gentle, something good deep down. The crazy part is that I still believe that. I really do." She shifted in bed and the arm-trapeze squeaked. "Okay, half-believe it."

Jake said, "I want to find him."

"You're crazy. Forget it."

"What's his last name?"

"You think I'm going to tell you? Give it up."

"I want to find out why he did this."

"Why? Come on, that would be the easy part. To Ace, you're either winning or you're losing. I dumped him, I threw him out. At that point he was losing. Now maybe he's the one that hurt me. He's winning again. So let's let it stay right there. He wins. Game over."

Jake shook his head so vigorously that his hair rose up above his ears. "No, that isn't good enough."

"For me it is."

"For me it isn't. Look, you can't have a world where people go around running each other over with speedboats and getting away with it."

"You can't? Except you do. Welcome to south Florida."

"But even here—"

"Even here, what? Listen, does it strike you as strange at all that the cops have shown like zero interest in what happened?"

Fumbling for an explanation, Jake said, "No one got a good look at the boat. They couldn't identify it."

"Or maybe they could," said Donna. "Maybe they know whose boat it was and they don't want to touch it. That ever occur to you?"

To Jake in his innocence it hadn't.

"The guy Ace works for, he's a powerful guy," she went on. "Ships stolen cars to South America. Turns the proceeds into drugs. Does loansharking. Has an arson and insurance racket. Spreads lots of money around. The cops leave him alone and Christ knows you should too."

"What's his name?"

"Jake, just stop! I'm not telling you his name and I don't want you getting involved."

Quietly but stubbornly, Jake said, "I'll find out who he is."

"Great, Sherlock. Do that. Then what? You start poking around and you end up in the hospital. Is that really what you want?"

She fixed him with a ferocious look but it was the word *hospital* that really got to him, imparted a queasy reality to the conversation, gave it the sour yellow smell of gore and the grinding texture of ripped ligaments and shattered bone. Playing off Jake's flustered silence, she pressed on. "Listen, I'm getting out of here tomorrow. Having some nice paid vacation. By next week I'll be doing physio. By next month I'll be good as new. No problemo. Like this fucking little mishap never happened. So will you please just leave it there?"

He thought about it for a moment, saw the bulge in her side where her wound was dressed, heard the little hamster-wheel squeak of the swing from which her arm was suspended. Then he said, "No. I'm sorry but I can't. I can't just leave it there."

22

Riding a taxi back to town, Jake found Joey Goldman's business card in his wallet and called him up. After a brief exchange of pleasantries, he said, "Joey, I have kind of a strange question for you. I'm trying to find somebody. Or somebody's name at least. Donna's old boyfriend's boss. I think he's some kind of gangster in Miami."

Not exactly defensively but certainly not without a bit of caution, Joey said, "What makes you think I'd know?"

With equal discretion, Jake said, "You just seem to know what's what down here. And your old friend Bert—"

"You trying to play detective or something?"

"No. Maybe. Sort of."

"So who is this guy you're looking for?"

"Some bigshot. Ships stolen cars, burns down buildings—"

Joey cut him off. "Whoa, whoa. You don't talk about shit like this on the telephone. That's pretty basic, Jake."

"Sorry. I'm learning as I go along."

"You had lunch yet?"

Jake said that he hadn't. He hadn't even noticed it was lunchtime.

"Meet me at the Eclipse Saloon. You know the place?"

Jake said that he didn't.

"Simonton Street. Ask any local. See you there in half an hour."

On the set of *Adrift*, Claire and Jacqueline Mayfield, the publicist, were standing on the periphery, witnessing what had been a rather sluggish and out-of-rhythm morning, rather like the first day back at school after a long vacation. Even though only a single day of shooting had been skipped, a certain momentum had been lost, the flow interrupted. Actors had a tough time finding their tone, honing their gestures, recapturing the attitudes they'd seemed to have mastered weeks before. Take after take was shot and discarded or just hacked off at some failed point in the middle.

It didn't help that Candace McBride kept muffing her lines.

Now and then she missed a cue. Once she skipped a speech ahead so that the conversation made no sense. Other times she faked it, just plain guessing at what her line might be. Once or twice she opened her mouth and nothing came out.

Finally, having yelled *Cut* for what seemed to him the hundredth time that day, the director gave vent to his exasperation. He stormed over to his diva, holding some papers high above his head and waving them in a quick tight circle.

"Candace, my dear, you see these pages? Collectively, they are called a script. The script is made of words. Your job is to memorize those words and speak them in a certain predetermined sequence with your fellow actors. Can you try to do that for me, Candace? Please?"

At that point Candace lost it.

Her losing it was not especially surprising. It happened often. But even by the star's high standards this was a spectacular meltdown. She snarled, she flared her nostrils, she balled her fists and stamped her feet. She hissed and mocked, but what was different about this outburst was that it seemed aimed not just at the director who'd dared to scold her, but at everyone around her. "Listen, you little asshole," she began, "you count for nothing, there are ten thousand hungry little B-listers who could do your job, and I am carrying this show. That's right, carrying it. On the screen and now in all these fucking interviews. I'm the one that people want to see. I'm up at fucking dawn, working at midnight, shilling my guts out while the rest of you are…what? Eating lobsters, chasing little boys? You don't know the strain I'm under. I barely had time to look at the piece of shit script, let alone memorize it. You can all go straight to hell for all I care."

And she bolted through the mangroves and the palm trees toward her tent.

For a moment no one breathed. Jacqueline Mayfield said very softly to Claire, "Christ, I've created a monster."

"No," Claire said. "She was a monster already. But you've definitely made it worse."

"Sounds like Charlie Ponte," Bert was saying. "Don't you think it sounds like Charlie Ponte?"

"Hey, you're the maven," Joey said, "but yeah, to me it sounds like Ponte."

Jake said nothing, just swiveled his head from one of them to the other and thought about the name. The syllables alone seemed a little frightening. Charlie Ponte. The hard consonants, the curt rhythm; it sounded like something being beaten with a pipe.

They were sitting at the bar at the Eclipse Saloon, near a wall festooned with dead mounted sailfish and tarpon, eating grouper sandwiches that leaked slivers of onion and bits of mushroom from the edges of the roll. They'd chosen the bar rather than a table so Bert could sneak in his dog. Dogs were not allowed but Bert had snuck his in for as long as anybody could remember. Everybody knew the dog was there, nestled in Bert's lap beneath the overhanging padded lip of the bar; nobody seemed to care.

"Course," the old man resumed, "just saying that it's Ponte, what the fuck does that do for us? It's not like we could just drop by or call him up."

"Why not?" said Jake.

"Why not?" echoed Bert. He seemed to find the question funny. He shared it with the dog. "Ya hear that, Giovanni? Our friend here wants to know why not." To Jake he said, "Just isn't how it's done. Ponte, he's old school. You want to talk to him, you set up a meet. Which isn't easy. Has so many bodyguards, his bodyguards have bodyguards. You talk to this guy, that guy, maybe eventually you get to Ponte. And after all that, why should Ponte give a shit?"

Jake said, "If he's so old school, he probably wouldn't approve of one of his guys running over an innocent woman with a boat. There's rules, right?"

"That's a point," Bert said. "There's rules. If anybody follows 'em anymore."

Joey put his sandwich down and fastidiously wiped his fingers on a paper napkin. "Can we please back up a step? You don't know for sure that the boyfriend did it. If he did do it, he's not gonna appreciate you snooping around. And who's Ponte gonna side with—a guy who's been loyal to him or someone he doesn't know from Adam?"

Bert thoughtfully stroked the chihuahua in his lap. "That's also a point."

Jake said, "I just want to find out if he did it."

Joey said, "Okay. Fine. Then what?"

For that Jake had no answer. The simple truth was that he hadn't thought that far ahead.

"You see, this is exactly the problem," Joey went on. "This is why this whole thing is a very bad idea. You can't just *find out*. You find out and then you're supposed to *do* something. And there's no good choices for what you'd do. You make a stink with Ace, he breaks your legs. You go to the cops, Ponte has you whacked. These are not good options."

With a steadfastness that surprised himself, Jake said, "I'll figure something out."

Off the beat, two-thirds of a moment later, Bert murmured, "Guy has balls. I didn't think he did but he does." He seemed to be saying it to the dog, to the fish on the walls, possibly to Joey, to everyone except Jake.

Joey took one more shot at talking Jake out of it. "Something like this, you start it, at some point you can't control it anymore."

Jake silently held his ground.

Out of rhythm but firmly, Bert said, "You want me to, I'll try setting up a meet. Might take a day or two. You mind driving to Miami?"

23

"Knock, knock," said Claire.

She was standing in front of Candace's tent, the Keys equivalent of the standard actor's trailer. The flaps were zipped tightly shut. Nearby, bugs were buzzing, palm fronds were rattling, but no sound was coming from inside.

After a moment, a voice asked who was there. It was Candace's voice but it was different now. The fire and the hiss had gone out of it. It was a soft and unsure voice, girlish and pouty.

Claire announced herself. The zipper came up with a rasp and Candace stepped aside to let her in. Then she quickly sealed the flap again and sat down on a cot, Claire sitting opposite. In the greenish filtered light inside the tent, she could see that the actress had been crying. In itself this was not a novelty. Candace summoned tears quite easily and often, both in her television role and in her tempestuous dealings with the world. Still, to Claire it was surprising and even touching to see that Candace might cry with no one watching, might cry just because she needed to.

Reaching out across the narrow space between them, Claire stroked the other woman's hand and said, "It's all right. Everybody's tired. Everyone was ready for a break."

Candace didn't answer right away. Like a child she just narrowed her eyes, looked down, and shook her head. Finally she said, "No, I went too far this time. I said some pretty awful things. Everyone'll hate me now."

The fact that no one had been too damn fond of Candace to begin with only made the remark more painful. Claire said, "It'll blow over. These things always do."

"I'm just so stressed out."

"I know, I know. The accident, the interviews–"

"It isn't only that," said Candace. Tightly gripping the edge of the cot with both hands, she'd pulled herself forward into an urgent posture. Her voice had become a confidential whisper, but a whisper that carried; a stage whisper. To Claire it seemed that, in a heartbeat, the actress had slammed shut the briefly opened window into her true emotions and was back to being a performer putting over a line. She paused a pregnant moment for effect, then said, "I think I'm being stalked."

Claire strained to keep her expression completely neutral but she remembered only too well the sick game-playing of a couple of evenings before, at the meeting with the suits. Now it seemed the diva was crying wolf again, creating yet more manipulative drama, probably meant to justify her tantrum.

Claire's skepticism must have shown, because Candace addressed it head-on. "Look, this has nothing to do with publicity or media or any of that nonsense. It just started yesterday. I look up and someone's there. Three, four times it's happened. Getting out of the limo. Leaving the hotel. Someone's standing not too far away, just staring at me, a really creepy stare. No expression, never looks away. Just watches."

Trying to be comforting, Claire said, "You know how it is around a show. There's always some fans who are a little weird, some harmless loser guys who have a crush on you."

"No, I know those types. I smile at them and they melt. This is different."

"Probably just a paparazzo then."

"No," said Candace. "There's no cameras. And it's a woman."

"A woman?"

"A blonde. Very tall, very stylish, very showy. Big sunglasses, sort of an orangey tint."

Suddenly a notch less skeptical, Claire said, "And sandals that lace up almost to her knees?"

Surprised, hopeful, Candace said, "Yeah, that's her. You know her?"

"I've seen her by the pool."

"*Our* pool?"

Claire nodded. "We said hello. I tried to be friendly. She's an oddball, that's all."

Candace was not persuaded. "It's more than that. The way she looks at me, it scares me."

Claire found nothing to say.

"The weirdest part," the actress went on, "is that she sort of looks familiar. Just vaguely. I can't place why. The hair? The posture? Something."

Claire admitted that she had had the same uneasy impression.

"That creeps me out," said Candace. "It really does." Her lower lip was trembling slightly. It was impossible to tell if the quivering was caused by skill or fear, or if her imploring tone was produced by anxiety or training. "Please, Claire, do something for me. Please. I don't know if I can stay here if you don't. Find out who that woman is."

24

In his ocean-view apartment at the Paradiso Condominium, Bert d'Ambrosia still possessed a telephone that was actually wired to the wall and whose receiver was connected to the dialing part by a twisted, curling cord. The phone was of a piece with the other furnishings, giving his place the feel of a consignment shop featuring artifacts from half a century ago. A Danish modern sofa. Space-age lamps. A formica kitchen table with a pattern of turquoise and coral boomerangs. There were a few pictures on the walls—seascapes, moonlit palms—and some photos of his long-dead wife in leaning frames on the end tables.

Bert now used his antique phone to try to reach some goombahs he used to know, hoping to recruit their help in setting up a meet with Charlie Ponte. He wasn't quite sure why he was bothering to do this. Partly as a favor to Jake, of course. But beyond that? Maybe he was just giving himself something to do, to think about. Wanting to remember what it was like to be part of things, a player, connected to the world beyond his ancient furniture and misnamed dog.

If that was the aim, the early results were disheartening. A few of the numbers he tried were either out of service or now belonged to people speaking languages he couldn't understand. Of the former associates he did manage to reach, a couple expressed frank amazement that Bert was still alive. They claimed to be happy to hear from him but could or would do nothing for him. With Charlie Ponte, everything came down to favors granted and favors owed; why waste a favor on an old man who hadn't mattered much for decades?

In his own mind, Bert was becoming embarrassed. He'd told Jake and Joey he could do this. He'd believed it himself. What if he couldn't get it done? How would he explain his failure? Sensing its master's subtle agitation, the chihuahua grew antsy as well. It started running manic circuits around the living room, past the torch lamp, underneath the breakfront, stopping now and then to sniff at pee stains left eons before by its predecessor, seeming to contemplate the archaic vapors as if they held the key to some crucial and abiding mystery.

Bert kept making calls.

Paolo, the front desk clerk at The Nest, was a sunny young man with stiff blonde hair above coal-black eyebrows and hollow disks the size of dimes in both his earlobes. Over the preceding weeks and months he'd worked up a deliciously gossipy rapport with Claire Segal, since she was the babysitter who'd settle up the cast members' bills if they flaked out, who'd pay for their breakage of glassware and pillaging of mini-bars, who'd apologize for their occasionally drunken or boorish behavior toward staff and other guests. He would have liked to answer her questions about the tall strange woman with the crazy sandals, but all he knew was that she'd checked out just an hour or so before.

"You know her name?" Claire asked.

Paolo looked discreetly around, past the potted ficuses and the vases filled with hibiscus blooms, and spoke softly. "I know the name she registered under. But it's obviously fake. Sorda Randy."

"Say again?"

He did.

"Spell it."

He did.

"That's a ridiculous name."

"Agreed," said Paolo. "But it's funny, whenever people use fake names, like if it's a closeted guy down here for a fling, they're almost always really ridiculous. Either like *John Smith* or something over the top, something made up after a few too many drinks. Like people want you to know they're playing games. Like *look at me, I'm being naughty*. People are funny, right?"

"Hilarious."

"Actually," said Paolo, "I thought that woman was with the show. She seemed so L.A."

"I thought so too. She said she wasn't from there."

"Ah, so you spoke with her."

"For about two seconds. It was strange. She drew my eye then cut me off."

"I know the type," said Paolo. "*Stare at me, be fascinated, but leave me alone*. Some weird power game."

"Well anyway," Claire said hopefully, "I guess she's gone now."

"I wouldn't bet on it."

"You just told me she checked out."

"Right. But she didn't look like she was leaving town."

"How does leaving town make people look?"

"Well, usually they're dressed for sitting on a plane. Which she wasn't. But okay, leave that aside. It's more something in their eyes. Like you can almost see their brain switching gears, already forgetting their time down here and thinking about where they're going back to and what they have to do there. You know, they're gone before they're gone. She didn't look that way. Her eyes were totally still here."

Claire considered, then said, "You spend a lot of time observing people, don't you?"

"What else I have to do all day? Oh, and one other thing about this woman. Her bag was really heavy. For its size, I mean. It was just a soft little shoulder kind of bag, but it was heavy. And she didn't seem to like me touching it. I lifted it, you know, just to hand it to her, but she grabbed it away."

"Any idea what was in the bag?"

Paolo shrugged. "You know better than I do what a woman traveling alone might carry in her bag. But it was way heavier than a lipstick, I'll tell you that."

25

Bert had worked the phone for a couple of dispiriting hours be-fore he finally reached a sentimental hit-man who agreed to help him out. The problem then was that he helped him out too well, too efficiently. He called Bert back within five minutes and told him that Ponte would meet with him and his friend at seven o'clock that evening. That was barely three and a half hours from the current time and it took nearly that long to drive from Key West to Miami.

Bert was suddenly in a major hurry. To be almost ninety and in a major hurry is not a healthy combination. Blood pounds in veins whose walls have worn thin. Objects get fuzzy at the edges and floors no longer seem quite flat. Bert blinked away the lightheaded-ness and called Joey. Joey called Jake. Jake swallowed hard but there wasn't enough time for fear to really build. He asked if Joey would be coming along. Joey declined; he'd met Ponte before and didn't care to repeat the experience. Jake said he'd rent a car. Joey said there wasn't time for that. He should take the El Dorado.

So it happened that late one January afternoon a ghostwriter from New York, who'd written on many subjects but never crime or criminals, and who in fact had never knowingly met a criminal until the day before, was driving a thirty-year old Cadillac convert-ible, top-down, muffler rumbling, in the company of an ancient Mafioso and his fussy little dog, en route to a sitdown with a noto-riously callous Mob boss, where he intended to accuse one of the boss's loyal soldiers of an out-of-bounds and cowardly act that he himself, however vaguely, intended to avenge or at the very least unmask.

Around twenty miles up the Keys, as if he was reading Jake's own thoughts, Bert said, "Ya sure ya wanna do this, kid?"

Jake glanced briefly at him, said nothing, kept driving. The tires crunched over the tiny bits of coral debris that always found their way onto the road.

"Ya want, we can turn around."

Jake said nothing for fear that his voice would sound terrified or otherwise bizarre. He just hunkered into the El Dorado's cushy seat and drove. The sun was behind them, putting fierce glints on certain facets of tin roofs. Tiny inlets inched in from the Gulf; here and there they all but lapped at the edge of the highway.

"Ya know the rules, at least?" Bert asked.

Jake admitted that he didn't.

"First rule: Be polite. Call him Mr. Ponte. Don't talk tough, you'll sound ridiculous. Don't ever mention the police. Got it?"

"Got it."

"Second: Very important. Always remember the whaddyacallit, the psychology of the situation. Ponte's a dick. A selfish bastard. But he's seen the *Godfather* movies. They all have. So he likes to see himself as like some kinda sawed-off Marlon Brando, a righter of wrongs. Kiss his ass on that, he'll like it."

"Got it."

Jake waited for additional advice, but Bert said nothing more. After a few minutes the younger man glanced over and saw that his passenger had fallen asleep. His head had rolled back against the cracked leather headrest and air was whistling peacefully through his enormous nose. The dog was napping too, serene in the fragrant paradise of its master's lap.

At the foot of Seven Mile Bridge, the El Dorado roared against the incline like an old propeller plane on a shallow takeoff. Jake was halfway to Miami.

Three short three blocks from The Nest, in an alley off of Whitehead Street, there was a guesthouse called Hannah's Hideaway, whose quaint pale-yellow Victorian exterior, with its chastely curtained windows and elaborately innocent gingerbread, served either as camouflage for, or ironic comment regarding, the highly permissive and varied goings-on inside. At this secretly rollicking hostelry, the tall blonde woman with the amber sunglasses was now checking in.

Once again she used an assumed name, though this time a far less colorful one: Jane Evans. Once again she laid down a substantial deposit in cash and once again she declined to show a credit card or driver's license. It was Key West and it was a tough economy and no one could afford to turn down business.

Having registered, she strolled through an oasis of a courtyard toward her room. Nude men, glistening like ducks on a rotisserie, lay sun-crisped on poolside lounges; their oiled body hair flashed like tinsel too near a lamp and about to catch fire. A pair of tattooed women luxuriated in a hot tub, rubbing tension from each other's shoulders, cooing in a language that seemed to be Sanskrit. The sensual hijinks seemed to mean nothing to the tall blonde woman. She kept a steady pace as she passed the pool and let herself into a small cottage behind a low hibiscus hedge.

She locked the door behind her, pulled the curtains tightly shut, and sat down on the bed, cradling her small bag between her knees. Reaching in, she produced a small silver picture frame closed up with a garnet clasp. Carefully she opened it so that it would stand up on her bedside table. In the frame was a photo of a handsome young man. He carried a surfboard under his arm and seemed just that moment to have emerged from the sea. His hair was wet and stiff with salt, droplets shone on the faint stubble of his chin. He both did and did not resemble the woman who so lovingly displayed his picture. His features were his own, but the structure of his face—the placement of the eyes, the angle of the jaw—might almost have been traced from hers.

Reaching into her bag a second time, she came out with a gun. It was not a ladies' gun and it was not a fancy gun—just an ugly, stubby .38 Police Special with a dull blue-black finish and a few scuffs on the butt. She'd bought it second- or third- or fourth-hand from a shop in East Los Angeles, and she'd chosen it because it was like the one that the young man in the photograph had used to kill himself.

She lifted the gun, placed the muzzle gently, almost caressingly, in the soft hollow beneath her ear, as she imagined the suicide must have also done. Then she pulled it away and sighted down its short barrel at the idle TV set in a corner of the room. Teasing herself with a phantom squeeze of the trigger, she made a dry clicking sound at the back of her throat, then put the weapon in her room safe and went outside to have a swim.

26

"What're you, some kinda wannabe detective?"

"No, Mr. Ponte. Not at all."

They were sitting in the boss's enormous office. Behind the wall of windows, a lingering pink dusk was painted on the sky above Biscayne Bay; the water underneath it was lifted in shallow folds and spattered with color like a dropcloth. Jake and Bert had been met at the twenty-second floor landing by a pair of bodyguards, then passed along to a second team of goons who'd stopped them in an anteroom and patted them down. This was a quite different pat-down from the bashful tickle-sessions Jake had occasionally experienced at airports. Here it was meaty hands clawing at his armpits, gasping at his legs, poking into the crannies of his groin and probing the cleft between his buttocks. By the time he was passed along to the inner sanctum he felt like he'd had some sort of deranged massage.

"What then?" Ponte went on. "Lemme guess: You've got a wrong to right and you think I'm Marlon Brando."

Jake could not help glancing at Bert, and Ponte shrewdly followed his eyes.

With a laugh the boss said, "I knew it! I knew that line of bullshit would come from the old man! Good ol' Bert the Shirt. Love ya, ya old bastard. *Here's how to get around Cholly Ponte: Make him feel like Marlon Brando.* 'Cept Bert, you're the last guy in America who still believes in that Crusader Rabbit shit. The rest of us, we're just trying to make a living and get through the day. But okay, kid, you're here. Tell me what's on your mind."

Jake fumbled a moment, trying to decide where to start, and during that interval Ponte suddenly noticed the chihuahua nestled in Bert's lap. "Bert," he said, "you got a new dog."

"Same dog."

"Same dog my ass. That other dog'd be like forty years old by now."

"Same dog."

There was an effort toward certainty in Bert's voice but a slight veil of confusion in his eyes, and Jake cut in to try to rescue him.

"Mr. Ponte," he said, "the other day there was an accident down near Key West. A woman got run over by a speedboat."

"Broad from the TV show, right? I think I saw something on the news."

"Right."

"Ya hosin' her?"

"Excuse me?"

"The broad who got run over. Ya boinkin' her?"

"No. She's just a friend. An acquaintance, really."

"So what's it to you she got run over?"

"I saw it happen."

"Yeah. So?"

"It just wasn't right, that's all."

"Lotsa shit ain't right. What of it?"

Jake squirmed, intensely aware of the large thug positioned behind his chair, and carefully considered his phrasing. As he was considering it, Bert jumped in to help him out.

"My friend here, he ain't makin' any accusations, but one of your guys, Ace his name is, used to be this woman's boyfriend till she threw him out on his ass, so we're wondering if maybe in any slight or incidental way he might have been involved in her misfortune."

"That's not an accusation?" Ponte said. "To me it sounds a great deal like an accusation."

"Okay, it's a little like an accusation," Jake admitted. "But it's no reflection on you, Mr. Ponte."

Unfortunately, at that moment Bert drifted off into one of his tangential thoughts that came blurting out an instant off the beat. "Though of course he would've had to get a boat from somewhere."

Ponte's face hardened. The change at first was nothing more than a slight adjustment to the crinkles at the outside corners of his eyes. He said, "Bert, we're old friends and all, but watch yourself."

Undaunted or perhaps just oblivious, Bert kept tracking his own line of thought. "I mean, a guy at Ace's level, he's not gonna have a half-mil speedboat to call his own."

"Shut up, old man. I mean it." The boss was glaring now and pointing a thick finger at Bert's face.

Softly, Jake said, "Can we please back up a minute, Mr. Ponte? Forget the accusations. All I'm asking from you is to help me find Ace so I can talk to him."

At this simple comment the thug behind Jake's chair began to laugh. His laugh was a sporadic, high-pitched titter like an oboe with a splintered reed and it was wildly incongruous coming from his massive body. Jake could not help swiveling toward him and saying, "What's funny?"

"You wanna talk to Ace. That's funny."

Ponte seemed to welcome this touch of levity and forced himself to smile along. "How much you weigh, kid?"

"One-sixty, one-sixty-five."

"You lift weights, anything like that?"

Jake just sat there feeling rather insubstantial.

"I didn't think so," Ponte said. "Ace goes two-fifty. I've seen him bench press three-twenty-five. I've also seen him break a guy's arm so bad that he could scratch his elbow with his thumb. If he had a thumb. And you just wanna have a friendly little chat with him about whether he almost killed his girlfriend?"

Jake had trouble coming up with a reply.

Ponte paused a moment then resumed. "You don't talk to Ace. *I'll* talk to Ace."

Again Jake found no ready words and Ponte went on as if airing out hurt feelings. "That's right. Me. I'll deal with it. You think I'd condone that kind of shit? You think that kind of shit would fly with me?"

Seeming to emerge from a trance, Bert said, "See. I told you he was old school. I said he was."

Ponte ignored him and said to his goons, "Any a you cheesedicks know where Ace is?"

There was a silence in which an array of uncertain and guilty glances panned across the room. Finally one of the thugs walked over and whispered something in Ponte's ear.

Ponte said, "Ya sure?"

The goon nodded that he was.

Ponte said, "That doesn't sound good."

The goon shrugged.

Ponte said casually, "Too late, kid. Your little mercy mission. Sweet idea, I respect it, but too late. Guy says Ace headed to Key West an hour ago. Said he had some unfinished business to attend to."

Without realizing he was getting up, Jake found himself halfway out of his chair. The goon pushed him back down into it again. "Mr. Ponte, he'll kill her. Someone's got to stop him."

Ponte raised his hands, fending off responsibility.

"You said you'd help! Two minutes ago. You promised."

"Don't tell me what I promised. That is never a good idea. I said I'd talk to him. I didn't say I'd chase him up and down the state of Florida. I got a business to run here. Priorities. I got people to see."

"And that's more important than someone getting killed?"

Without hesitation Ponte said, "Way more."

Jake bit his lower lip and squeezed the arms of his chair. "Okay. Okay. I'll find him myself. I'll deal with him myself."

Once again he started rising from his chair and this time the bodyguard let him. Ponte shot him a sort of valedictory glance and said, "I wish you well, kid. I really do. You got Blue Cross?"

27

Jake gunned the engine of the El Dorado.

The car was still parked in front of Charlie Ponte's condo, not in gear, and of course it went nowhere. Still, there was a kind of release in high-revving the archaic old V-8, hearing the roar, feeling the quiver of the chassis as the gas exploded in the cylinders and the pistons slammed in their exigent rhythm, straining the rivets in the engine block. The brief and rising roar suggested assertion and decisiveness. Then it dwindled into a softly clattering purr as the motor returned to idle, and Jake sat there in the driver's seat feeling rather helpless. "Shit, Bert," he said. "Guy's got an hour head start. Now what do I do?"

Sitting somewhat slumped on the passenger side, Bert contemplatively stroked the head of his chihuahua as if he was rubbing his own chin. "Broad's still inna hospital, right?"

"She gets out tomorrow morning."

"That's okay then," the old man said. "Nothin's gonna happen while she's inna hospital."

"You sure?"

"My age, I ain't sure of nothin'. But I'm pretty sure. I'd say we got all night to find him."

"We?"

"Hey, I don't sleep good anyway. Ya gotta be awake, ya might as well be doin' somethin', right?"

Jake didn't so much consider the comment as absorb it. *Might as well be doing something.* Well, of course. Doing *anything.* Action! That was the key, he realized–the key to beating back helplessness, refreshing his resolve. Just *do* something, then do something else, and something else again, until decisive action became a habit and a reflex that might actually lead to results and maybe even pass for courage. He put the giant car in gear and, showing off for no one but himself, burned rubber as he headed back down the Keys.

By that time, Charlie Ponte's enormous desk was almost entirely covered in money.

The money had been poured forth from a black satchel carried by the boss's next appointment, a very handsome man whose perfect salt-and-pepper hair rose and fell in elegant, old-fashioned finger waves. The bills were all crisp new fifties neatly bundled into stacks of twenty. There were two hundred packets in all, and the payment represented a small fraction of what Ponte would realize from a relatively modest investment in an independent film that had caught on. He stared down at the cheery profusion of cash and smiled. He had never lost his zest for making money and in this he was a fortunate man. "These Hollywood deals," he said, "when they pay off they pay off good."

"Nature of the business," said Handsome Johnny Burke. "High risk, high reward."

"The reward part I like," said Ponte.

"Plus it's totally legit," Johnny added.

Which was true if you chose to overlook a couple of inconvenient facts, such as that the money that Ponte channeled into movie projects had originally been obtained through theft, extortion, and occasionally murder. Still, by the time the profits had been filtered through a fancy L.A. law firm and the experienced bookkeepers at Handsome Johnny's Crab Joint, the money had been scrubbed quite clean. But again, on the less savory side of the ledger, Ponte seemed to regard the funds he tendered as either investments or loans, depending entirely on his own advantage. If a movie succeeded, the Miami boss counted himself as a savvy investor and took a goodly cut of the box office. If it tanked, he regarded his stake as a loan that needed to be paid back anyway. The lawyers and accountants tried tactfully to point out the illogic of this position, but to Ponte it made perfect sense, and it was Ponte's money, after all.

With the payoff piled right there on the desk between them, Handsome Johnny seized an opportunity to remind the other man of his value to him. "My West Coast connections," he said. "Been working pretty sweet."

Not wanting his sometime business partner to feel too good about himself, Ponte said, "Course, you've brought me some real duds, too."

His toothsome smile tightening just slightly, Johnny said once again, "Nature of the business."

"Like that fucking genius who killed himself. Why'd you have me invest in a suicidal lunatic? Total loss on that one."

Suddenly solemn, Johnny said, "A tragedy."

"For who?" said Ponte. "Him or me? Schmuck blows his brains out, I'm out half a million bucks." The boss wagged his head sadly then grew philosophical. "Besides, what kind of asshole kills himself at thirty? Unless he gets whacked he's got his whole life in front of him. The beach. Pussy. Food. Beautiful things. Okay, he's got some problems. Who doesn't? But what a fucking cop-out. Play your hand, man! You lose, you lose. Am I right or am I right?"

"You're right," said Johnny.

Getting back to business, Ponte said, "And I don't really buy this crap that we can't collect just because the fucking guy is dead."

Handsome Johnny shrugged. "He spent the money. Legitimately. On the movie. The accountants have a record of it. Location scouting. Promos. Guarantees to actors. He spent it. It's gone."

The notion of his money being gone, the seeming finality of it, offended Ponte and he suddenly went from being philosophical to starting to get angry. Earlier in the conversation he really hadn't been. Thorny, maybe, but not yet angry. But that's how anger was with him; it came on without much warning, like gas pains, and he himself could not control it or even say exactly why it had been triggered at a certain juncture and not another. Now he twined his fingers, turned his palms away, and pressed outward till the knuckles cracked. "There's gotta be a way to get that money back. Some of it, at least."

"Sorry, but I just don't think there is. Let it go. You'll more than make it up on this other movie."

That did not satisfy Ponte. "Ain't there someone we can squeeze?"

"Who? This director, this Bouchard, he took the money on his own. It was his loan, his deal. There was no one else involved."

"There's gotta somebody who'll make good. Family? Wife? Girlfriend?"

Handsome Johnny didn't want to go there. "Charlie, please, it isn't worth the bother."

"Getting paid is always worth the bother."

"Even from a dead guy?"

"Not everybody's dead. Find me someone we can squeeze."

"But Charlie—"

Ponte cut him off. He'd made up his mind. It was his money and someone had to pay it back. "There's gotta be somebody. There always is."

28

The small bar at The Nest was called Nellie's and it was very different from most of Key West's other bars. It was quiet; it was decorous. There was no live music, no stale beer smell, no Jimmy Buffett songs playing on the soundtrack. At Nellie's you could have a peaceful drink without hearing the loud life story of someone who'd moved down years before from Michigan and how it was the best thing that he ever did, and on and on and on.

Nellie's was where Candace McBride had most of her dinners. Sometimes another cast member joined her, seldom the same cast member more than once, but usually she ate alone, sipping Chardonnay, picking at shrimp. The bartenders handled her perfectly. They made it clear that they recognized her as a star and then they backed off, waiting for clues as to what she needed from them at a given moment. If she needed to be fussed over, they fussed. If she needed to be left alone, they polished glasses and acted like she wasn't there. Candace badly needed a place like that, a place that suited her many moods and in fact adjusted itself, like lighting on a stage, in accordance with them.

But now that she was being stalked, she feared that even this cozy and inviolate hiding place might be spoiled for her. What if the weird blonde woman suddenly came walking in to stare at her? To *see* her in a way that no one else seemed able to, to look right past the artifice and the willed impressions to who and what she really was. That sense of truly being seen was what she found so supremely unsettling in the woman's unremitting gaze; the mere thought of it put a jumpy feeling in her legs, made her hands feel tight and clammy. Sitting at a corner of the bar where no one could move up behind her, her eyes darted left and right, searching for an enemy.

When Claire came in to find her, she was on her third glass of wine and was rather listlessly pushing some lettuce leaves around a plate. "Mind if I join you?"

"Please," said the actress. "I'd love some company."

Climbing onto the barstool next to her, Claire ordered a gin and tonic and asked how she was feeling. A hint of a wistful smile in gratitude for being asked was quickly followed by a narrowing of her violet eyes to convey that she was still troubled. "Not having my easiest day."

"Well, I have some excellent news for you. The woman who's been bothering you has checked out."

Candace dropped her fork and grabbed Claire's forearm. "Oh, that's great. I'm so relieved. She's left town?"

Claire hesitated, hedged. "I guess so."

Brightening as though a spotlight was being ratcheted up in front of her, Candace said, "So tell me. How'd you find out? Who is she? What do we know about her?"

"I talked to a buddy at the desk. We don't know much. No real name or anything like that. But it doesn't matter. She's gone. And she's just a nut."

Candace couldn't quite accept such a blithe dismissal. "I don't know. The way she looked at me…"

Trying to keep things light, trying to ease the diva's mind, Claire said, "Just a nut, believe me. The desk guy thought so too. A harmless wacko. Who knows, maybe some kind of nymphomaniac or something. She used the most ridiculous fake name. Sorda Randy."

Claire said it with a laugh but it was clear at once that the joke fell flat.

"Randy?"

Awkwardly now, Claire said, "You know, old-fashioned word for horny. Sort of randy. Get it?"

"I used to date a guy named Randy," Candace said. "Randy Bouchard. Lived with him in fact."

Making one more attempt at leavening the moment, Claire said, "And did he live up to the billing?"

"He killed himself."

"Oh. I'm sorry," Claire said. Then, her memory jogged, she thought she recalled seeing, perhaps six months before, a brief item from the L.A. *Times* about the death. The usual paragraph about wasted promise, next to a slick publicity photo of someone talented, beautiful, and gone.

"I wasn't," said Candace. "I left him and he killed himself and I wasn't even sorry. Terrible, right? I was glad to have him out of the way. It would make things easier for me. That's what I thought at the time. Join me in another drink?"

A slight lift of her head was enough to summon the bartender from the soft shadows of his post. He took their order and slid away again.

"He loved me," Candace went on. "That was the problem. He said he loved me and he meant it. He wanted us to do great things together, make movies together. He was an upcoming writer and director. He started working on a new script as soon as we started dating. A love story, of course, for me to star in. Passionate. Sizzling. So intense it hurt. He worked on it for a year, then started showing it to the studios. No takers. It was too strange, too raw. But by then he was obsessed with it. He turned down other work, couldn't think of anything else. Finally he decided to make the movie on his own. He started borrowing money. I don't know where he got it, but we're not talking about the corner bank, okay? And it was money he'd never be able to pay back unless the film got made and was a hit."

The bartender brought the fresh drinks over then moved away as quietly as a geisha.

Claire said, "So then what happened?"

Candace sipped some Chardonnay before resuming. "I bailed."

"On him? On the movie?"

"Both. But in his mind they were the same thing. The movie was about our love affair. The love affair was about the movie. It was all tied up together. Exciting for a while. Probably fucked up too—this young genius making me his Muse. But meanwhile my career was going nowhere. I started losing faith. I started getting sick of waiting.

"Then, one night, I was at a party in Santa Monica and I heard about this new TV show being cast. They were looking for a fresh face, a relative unknown that they could make a star. And I thought: This is my chance. Mine. Not being anybody's Muse. Not being the other half of someone else's dream. So I auditioned and I got the part and I packed a bag and I walked out on Randy and his movie."

"He didn't see it coming?"

"Why would he? We hadn't fought. We still shared a bedroom. Most days we were happy. I just changed my mind. Made a different plan."

"Did you love him?"

Candace tried to smile but her neck sinews fluttered and the effect was more of a wince. "That's the thing," she said. "The awful thing. I don't know. I didn't know what it should feel like. I didn't know then and I don't know now."

Claire found nothing to say to that. She dropped her eyes, stirred her drink and fiddled with her slice of lime. In the quiet bar random noises filtered through the awkward pause—the squeak of a chair leg, the clink of glasses, a muffled laugh. Her mind started to wander, linking things that hadn't seemed related until then. A face that both looked familiar, and didn't. A preposterous pseudonym. Sorda Randy. Possibly as in *soeur de* Randy? Finally she said, "Your former boyfriend—he have a sister?"

29

It was after eleven when Jake and Bert and the dog made it back to town. They'd called Joey from the road, asked him to stake out the compound and let them know if Ace showed up. They'd heard nothing so they headed straight to Duval Street to search for him. Given the rush and tumult of the previous few days, Jake had not yet managed to get down there. Seeing the famously raucous and libidinous boulevard for the first time at eleven-thirty on a night in high season was somewhere between a tease, a tickle, and a full-scale madhouse assault.

Transvestite hookers vamped in red high heels with vertiginous platforms, fishnet stockings tracing out their lean and freshly shaven legs. Drunk young ladies from Southern colleges teetered by in wet sorority T-shirts, their hairdos wrecked and their nipples taut and finely crinkled like the pits of apricots. Biker guys lumbered past, their sleeveless leather vests festooned with studs and club regalia. Stirred in among the more colorful characters was an array of average-looking tourists, regular folks, some seeming amazed at what a good time they were having, some clinging to each other and looking meekly down as if they feared that too frank a gaze would turn them into pillars of salt. From a dozen doorways and patios blared bursts of competing music and manic laughter.

Bert led the way to Sloppy Joe's, with its big glassless windows and famous logo of Hemingway in a bulky turtleneck in which he must have sweltered. Inside the place, there were guys dressed up like pirates, with do-rags on their heads and gold hoops in their ears; there were guys tattooed in lavish colors and guys tattooed in basic indigo. There was a guy with a cockatiel, a guy with a monkey, a woman with a ferret that calmly nestled between her breasts. But there was no one who looked like a two hundred-fifty pound enforcer. Jake and Bert had one beer and left.

At Captain Tony's the crowd was slightly more sedate but also more leathery and cranky. Serious drinkers, sunshine etched deep into their corrugated hides. Maybe a neighborhood bully or two, but no goombahs.

Hog's Breath presented a row of silver ponytails and wizened backsides that seemed to have melted into their customary barstools. Rick's was full of kids firing down bizarre drinks made of things like jello and oyster juice; Margaritaville was populated mainly by women of a certain age pretending to be girls again, waiting for a pickup attempt if only for the nearly forgotten satisfaction of being asked and saying no. There was no sign of their quarry, and at one-thirty or so, with Bert sporadically nodding out and the tiny chihuahua yawning as widely as a hippopotamus, they gave up.

Jake drove Bert home, then went to the compound, where he found Joey lightly dozing in a poolside lounge. He'd seen no sign of Ace. Jake thanked him for the use of the car and handed him the keys. Joey wished him luck and left.

For a few moments the writer stood there alone by the pool. The night was very still, so quiet that he could hear insect wings spanking against nearby streetlights. The moon had set and the stars were softened in their twinkling by a gauze of humidity that was like the merest memory of a cloud. It was extraordinarily peaceful, and Jake, for the moment, felt peaceful too; in part at least because he knew there was more to be done and he had somehow become serene in the rather reckless belief that he could do it. He savored this fragile conviction for a few more fragrant breaths, then stepped around the pool to the shed where Bryce lived.

There was a line of pallid light beneath the ill-fitting door. Jake knocked very softly and Bryce immediately said, "Come in." He was lying on his bed beneath a fraying sheet, his elbows splayed across his pillows and his lightly laced fingers cradling his head.

Straddling the threshold of the shed, Jake said, "You're a trusting guy. You don't even ask who's there?"

Bryce said, "It's two o'clock in the morning, who's it gonna be?"

Jake said, "I thought you might be sleeping."

"I don't sleep that much at night," said Bryce. "Little catnaps now and then. Nights I mostly think."

"What about?"

"Stuff I might do sometime. Accomplishments. Adventures. Stuff like that."

"Ah," said Jake, and glanced at the random calendars tacked to the wall.

He said nothing more and after a moment Bryce asked, "Is there some particular reason you're stopping by?"

Jake hesitated. "I don't know if it's really fair to ask you."

Bryce sat up in bed. "Ask me, ask me."

"Okay," said Jake. "Remember when you said that if I was going to play detective, maybe you could be my helper?"

By way of answer, Bryce sat up higher and clawed at the confining sheet.

"Well here's your chance," Jake said.

30

Perhaps an hour of quiet waiting had gone by when Jake and Bryce first heard the pick scratching at the keyhole of Donna's cottage. Metal pressed metal deep in the works of the flimsy lock, then the doorknob turned with a small but grating squeak. There was a brief pause, a tiny rustling. A heartbeat later Ace's bulk was glutting up the doorway and he stepped heavily across the threshold.

From behind the open door, standing in near perfect darkness, Jake called out his name.

The big man swiveled toward the sound. Bryce sprang up from his hiding place behind the sofa and brained him with a Dustbuster. The blow caught Ace just aft of the crown of his head and was delivered with such force that the plastic casing of the small appliance shattered and flew off, leaving the suction motor and dirt bag exposed. Ace hovered for a moment, swaying in a lazy circle. Then he abruptly dropped to his knees and lingered briefly as though praying before pitching forward flat on his face at Jake's feet.

As he fell, something flew from his hands. Jake felt a tickle of almost weightless objects falling against his legs and insteps.

Bryce switched on a light and the two allies regarded their prostrate foe with the mute fascination that might greet the appearance of a dead shark washed up on a beach. His giant legs were folded at a restful angle. His bunched shoulders were lifted in a bewildered shrug. A small smudge of blood was visible through his hair at the point of impact. And what had fallen from his hands, and now lay spread across the floorboards and over Jake's sneakers, was a huge bouquet of assorted flowers. There were slightly wilted roses, curling lilies, irises that sagged. There were crinkly mums and sunflowers missing petals here and there.

Jake looked down at the incongruous and inexplicable array and felt a moment's doubt and remorse. He gingerly nudged Ace with his toe to see if he would move. He didn't. He said to Bryce, "Maybe you didn't need to hit him quite so hard."

Bryce still had the ruined Dustbuster in his hand. Absently, he plucked some lint from its filter. "Better too hard than not hard enough. What's up with the flowers?"

Jake said, "I have no idea." Very carefully, backing and sidling, he moved away from the scattered bouquet and the unconscious giant. "I guess we better tie him up."

PART 3

31

In Los Angeles it was only midnight, and Quentin Dole was still working. Sitting in his Santa Monica apartment, the damp light off the Pacific mingling with the designer halogen above his desk, he was sorting through a pile of ratings reports, magazine clippings, and media summaries, parsing the data in a dizzy-making effort to understand the tendencies and fickle desires of the viewing public.

What he had before him was infuriating but it painted no clear picture. By almost any measure, his and Jacqueline's strategy of portraying what had happened to Donna as possibly an abortive attempt on the life of Candace McBride had been a definite success. Candace had sold the story brilliantly and the press had bought it wholesale. She'd done nearly a dozen on-air interviews; her portrait graced the covers of several mass-market magazines; her name was all over the tabloids. And yet the ratings had actually gone down. Gone down, it's true, by the tiniest of increments, maybe just a statistical blip. Then again, it was by tiny increments, defections by a tiny fraction of the audience, that TV shows lost their cachet and eventually their time slot. What the hell was going on?

The driven producer whose future was glued to the success of the program racked his brains over the conundrum, and the best answer he could come up with was only another question: Was it possible that the public had become more interested in the melodrama surrounding the show than in the show itself? That the hype, on its own, had become more compelling than the product being touted? A fine irony that would be for a spinner of fictions-within-fictions, a creator of stories with stories of their own to tell.

Dole switched off the desk light, poured himself a scotch and popped a sleeping pill. His last thought before slipping off into a sporadic and uneasy sleep was that perhaps Candace McBride had rather suddenly become too big for her role, had gone from being his greatest asset to becoming a distraction and a liability. She was on the cusp of becoming bigger than the show, and this was not allowable. No one, with the possible exception of Quentin Dole himself, could be bigger than the show.

Also awake at that late hour was the strange blonde woman who'd arrived in Key West by speedboat and had set about trailing and tormenting the faithless, selfish actress who'd betrayed and destroyed her brother.

The blonde, whose true name was Marguerite Bouchard, was lying chastely in her bed at Hannah's Hideaway, reading. The big amber shades she wore by day had been replaced by a pair of simple reading glasses. The glasses, together with the felt-tip marker she held in her hand and the rather careless way her hair spread out on the pillow beneath her, gave her an aspect that was more scholarly than dangerous. She was reading not from a book but from a looseleaf binder such as people use at school; she might almost have been a grad student in literature, studying for exams. She read awhile, then stopped to underline or highlight or scribble notes in the margin. When she wrote, her tongue moved to the corner of her mouth in concentration.

After a while she put the notebook aside and got up out of bed. She pulled on her snug pants that buttoned just below the knee and strapped on her gladiator sandals. She squeezed into her tight leather jacket and grabbed the ignition key to her speedboat. It was an odd time to go for a boat ride, but the obsessed blonde woman had an errand to run that could only be accomplished while most of the world was sleeping. From the small fridge in her hotel room she took a glass jar with air holes punched in its dull metal top and headed for the marina.

32

In the roughly five minutes it took Ace to regain consciousness, Bryce had gathered up the scattered flowers, arranging them into a rather rustic yet artful bouquet. He hummed softly as he did so, like a clerk in a fancy florist's shop.

When the big man finally came to, he didn't wake up all at once. His bound ankles gave a twitch then were motionless again. His tied hands attempted to move away from the small of his back and seemed surprised that they could not accomplish this. He briefly raised his head but its weight was too much to support just yet and it fell back to the floor. At last he opened his eyes, blinking and squinting. His pupils were pinwheeling and his focus was smeared so that images were ghosted at the edges. Through the haze and glare he saw Jake sitting in a chair above him. "Who the fuck are you?" he slurred.

"Friend of Donna's. Live next door."

Ace considered this quite calmly. "Wha'd you hit me for?"

"I didn't."

Bryce got up from the sofa and came around where Ace could see him. Without malice but with a sort of bashful pride, he said, "I did."

Craning his neck, Ace said, "You scrawny little bastard. Just because I threw you in the pool?"

Bryce looked to Jake, who was trying to gather his thoughts. It was very late. He was exhausted, flummoxed by the flowers, and his certainty had begun to fade. Groping for a tone that suited the moment, he said gruffly, "Because you ran Donna over with a speedboat."

"I *what?*"

Hoping to sound confident and prosecutorial, Jake said, "Don't deny it. She dumped you and you ran her over."

"No I didn't."

The simplicity of the denial stymied Jake and he stalled in his interrogation.

Ace went on. "You guys have this totally ass backwards wrong."

Bryce jumped in and tried to help. "You took her script. I saw you take it."

The big man on the floor said, "Yeah, I took the script. What of it?"

Jake said, "You took it because it had the schedule so you'd know when she'd be in the water."

For the first time in the conversation the bound man seemed agitated. He kicked at the leg ropes, strained at the ones around his wrists. Miserably, he said, "I didn't know it had the schedule. I didn't know what would happen. If I knew what was gonna happen I never woulda took it."

"Why'd you take it then?" asked Bryce.

"That's none of your business. Come on, untie me."

"Why'd you take the script?" Jake pressed.

"It was a job, okay? Someone paid me."

"Who? Charlie Ponte?"

At the mention of the name, Ace stiffened as if tased. "How the fuck you know Ponte?"

"Never mind how. It was his speedboat you were driving, right?"

"Just to come down here and grab the notebook. Ponte didn't even know."

"Go on."

"Go on, what?"

"Then who'd you take the script for?"

"I don't know."

Warming to the cross-examination, Jake said, "Bullshit, you don't know. How could you not know?"

"Look, I got the job through a middle man. Said it was for some rich wacko fan. I didn't ask questions. What did I care? I got paid five grand and it was easy. Plus I was mad at Donna. That much I admit. But that was then, not now. Now lemme up off the fucking floor. My head hurts like a bastard."

"Who's the middle man?" Jake asked.

"What?"

"The guy who hired you to grab the script."

Ace shook his head as well as he could manage. "Don't go there. That's the kind of thing that gets people whacked. Leave it the fuck alone and let me up."

Jake looked at Bryce. Bryce looked at Jake. They were softening but they were still afraid to let the big man loose. "One more question first," Jake said. "The flowers."

"What about 'em?"

"Why you carrying flowers in the middle of the night?"

"Are you guys stupid or what? Why'm I carrying flowers. I'm carrying flowers 'cause Donna gets home tomorrow. I called the hospital."

"She won't want to see you," said Jake.

With surprising wistfulness, Ace said, "That's possible. I was a real jerk before. But I want her to have flowers to come home to. And I wanna take care of her. If she'll let me. Can't you understand that? Ain't you guys ever been in love?"

Ashamed, Jake and Bryce glanced over at the extravagant if slightly past its peak bouquet. In a conciliatory way, Bryce said, "That's a lot of flowers. Where you get 'em all, this hour?"

"The cemetery. Where else? Spent like three hours finding them in the fucking dark. Now will you assholes please untie me?"

33

For the cast and crew of *Adrift,* there was a five a.m. call for a scene scheduled to be shot at sunrise.

When the vans and limos, headlights sweeping, gathered on Big Sandy Key, the western sky was still a mystic purple pocked with stars, while in the east the seam between sea and heaven was just becoming visible, a tissue of dim haze shimmering between them like the dancing steam above a pot of heating water. Crickets rasped, frogs croaked, abrupt and fleeting splashes were faintly heard as the rays and crabs and fishes went about their secret pre-dawn business. The air was at its coolest and most damp; it seemed made of tiny droplets that burst and yielded up their moisture like bubbles in a drink to tickle skin and noses.

On the far side of the barge crossing, muttering and yawning, the crew began setting up the shot. It was to be filmed on a pretty arc of beach where wavelets sizzled softly through the knobs of coral and a single, perfect palm, iconic in its wind-bent posture and the serene but melancholy droop of its fronds, provided a perfect spot for rest and contemplation. Beneath this palm, Candace McBride would be sitting as the sun lifted from the sea. A male character named Beau—another hopeful suitor for the difficult and irresistible Lulu—would approach, and they would share a few lines of dialogue. It was a very simple scene, mainly a pretext to show Candace in a string bikini top, sitting barelegged and languorous as the slow, red, and fleshy light of dawn licked across her skin.

The eastern sky showed bruised green, then pale yellow, and the actors took their places, some dozen feet apart. The director waited for the sun to lift its shoulders from the ocean, then called for action.

BEAU
(raptly watching the sunrise, then noticing Lulu)
My very favorite place. Yours too?

She just nods dreamily. He looks at her with longing.

BEAU
What are you thinking?

LULU
Oh, nothing.
(a pause)
No, actually, what I was thinking...What I was thinking on such a gorgeous morning, is that if we never
got rescued, if we were out here forever...

A longer pause, as she looks flirtatiously at
Beau and leans back against the palm.

LULU
(cont'd)
...maybe it wouldn't really be so...

"*BAD!*" screamed Candace as she broke the scene and rocketed to her feet, jumping and stamping and reaching futilely around to slap at her bare back, from which a large brown scorpion, roughly the length and girth of a human index finger, was dangling and bobbing, still rooted in her flesh by the barbed and pulsing stinger squeezing out its venom. She howled, she cursed, she spun, and after a long, frozen moment Beau ran over and awkwardly swatted at the wriggling beast. The stinger pulled out with an almost audi- ble pop from the hole it had made in the diva's perfect skin, and

135

the scorpion fell to the ground, dying but not dead, curling spasmodically, flailing its nightmarish pincers. Candace looked down
at the horrible creature, felt its venom spreading fire between her
shoulder blades and behind her heart, and passed out on the coral.

Jake and Bryce had spent the balance of the night babysitting Ace,
still not quite comfortable at the thought of leaving him in Donna's
place without a chaperon. They took turns napping; now and then
they chatted, small talk mostly. At daybreak Bryce had made coffee and scavenged some bread from the freezer. The cottage filled
with the companionable smell of toast and the three men sat there
almost like old friends preparing to head out for an early shift of
work.

They'd been waiting many hours for Donna to appear, but when
she finally arrived at the compound—unannounced, delivered
from the hospital by taxi–they were oddly unprepared. The dishes
were undone, toast crumbs dotting the plates. The straggles of rope
with which Ace had been tied sat guiltily on a coffee table; the shattered and skeletal Dustbuster leaned against a wall. The men had
made no plan for how to welcome Donna home, and her entrance
was entirely undramatic.

The doorknob turned and she stood there in the doorway. She
was wearing a loose-fitting dress but even so it could be seen that her
somewhat swaggering athletic posture was compromised and tilted by
the tugging stitches in her healing wound. She was pale from three
days in a hospital bed and her right arm was in a sling. She seemed to
notice the vast bouquet of pilfered, fading flowers before she noticed
the three men. Then her eyes flicked past Jake and Bryce and settled
on her former lover, and the two of them just stared.

After a moment Ace said very gently, "Hello, baby."

Donna said nothing. Her mouth twitched in what might have
been a false start toward a tentative smile.

Looking at her arm, the cautious way she stood, Ace said, "You
been hurt." As he said it his hard black eyes welled up; the flinty
pupils smeared and the rims instantly grew red and puffy.

By way of answer, Donna said only, "It wasn't you?"

"Tell me you never thought that, baby."

"I did think it, Ace. Why wouldn't I? You used to scare me."

He looked down at the floor. "I'm so, so sorry for that. I never will again. These last few days, worrying about you, I've learned some things. I'm a different guy. I swear."

She considered that a moment, waited to see if the heartfelt sound of it would last or leak away into the intervening silence.

Ace went on, "Can I stay with you a while? Few days, at least?"

Donna said nothing.

"You're gonna need some help," he said. "Groceries and stuff. Cooking. Driving you around."

Donna took as deep a breath as her bandages allowed, pushed her lips out as she weighed the offer, then finally gave in to a slightly twisted smile into which she poured her gradually returning high spirits and ribaldry. "No sex, Ace. No way. I still got stitches. You know that, right?"

He nodded, almost shyly, and she moved slowly toward him, her good arm outstretched to circle him as she laid her cheek against his chest.

Jake and Bryce took the opportunity to slip out of the cottage. Near the pool, in the quickly mounting sunshine, they shared a sleepy and understated high-five then parted company and went off to get some sleep.

34

Jake didn't get to rest for long. Around ten o'clock his cell phone rang and woke him. It was Claire, telling him there'd been another mishap on the set. They needed to talk. Could he meet her up at Smathers Beach, somewhere between the shave ice stand and the pizza wagon?

He dragged himself out of bed and into a cool shower. He pulled on a bathing suit, rolled the purple bicycle out of the rack by the compound gate, and headed for the ocean. He rode shakily along the busy promenade, dodging skaters, joggers, people walking dogs that were frantically intoxicated with the wealth of salty smells.

He found Claire perched on a blanket that she'd laid out over the trucked-in sand. She was lying on her stomach, lifted up on her elbows so she could spot him and wave. The arc of her back was graceful and lithe. There was both strength and something poignant, breakable, in the way her shoulders pinched together beneath her glistening skin. She wore a one-piece bathing suit, chaste but elegant, black and snug. She shielded her eyes with her hand and said hello.

"I get to see you in your play clothes again," he said.

"Shooting's cancelled for the day. Thank God. I really need some time to myself."

"But I'm here," Jake observed.

"Yeah, but that's different. That's a good thing."

Still standing above her, he said, "So what happened on the set?"

She patted the empty space next to her. "Come share the blanket."

He lay down, not too close but close enough that he could feel the borrowed sunshine radiating from her side and legs and warming him. He smelled her sunscreen, that endlessly nostalgic sweet and coconutty smell that was a summary of so many perfect days and brought back muddled memories of every momentary crush he'd ever had on a woman at the beach. Settled beside her, he said, "We aren't on a date, right?"

She said, "We aren't on a date."

"Just making sure. So tell me what happened this morning."

She lowered her head, rested her cheek on the back of her hand, and sighed. "Well, it was Candace."

"Of course."

"Of course," Claire echoed. "But, you know, just because she's a narcissist and a paranoid, that doesn't mean she's wrong. She was badly stung by a scorpion."

Jake couldn't help wincing at the thought. "Nasty piece of luck," he said.

"Except it wasn't. Someone set it up."

"Set up a scorpion sting?"

She didn't answer, just reached into her beach bag and came out with a sheet of paper—half a sheet of paper, actually, hand-torn on a jagged diagonal. Handing it to Jake, she said, "I found this in the mangroves just a few feet from where it happened."

It was a page from the script. Not just any page. The page that had Candace on that beach and leaning back against the tree.

"So you think—"

"I googled scorpions," she said. "Amazing what you can learn in thirty seconds. They're nocturnal and photophobic. Hiding under foliage or loose tree bark where it's nice and dark and cool is one of their favorite things. Contrary to their reputation, they're not aggressive. They only sting if something threatens them. Like by leaning back and caving in the bark."

Jake considered and gradually, dimly noticed that his usual sense of what was possible was being altered, stretched, perhaps suspended altogether. This was Key West. If a speedboat could be used as a weapon, why not a scorpion? After a moment he said, "Careless, though, leaving the page behind."

Claire disagreed. "I don't think it was careless at all. I think it was left there on purpose. To freak out Candace even more. And I have a pretty good guess for who might have done it."

Jake made no effort to mask his surprise. "You do?"

"The sister of Candace's old boyfriend."

"Wait a second. The sister–?"

So Claire filled him on the story of the betrayal and the suicide and the stalking. "But still," she went on, "there's two things I can't figure. How she got a copy of the script. And how she planted the scorpion in the middle of the night."

Jake let his head rest on the blanket. The warm sand seemed to loosen up his brain and something clicked. He said, "Hold on. I bet I know how she got the script. Donna's boyfriend stole it for her. Except he didn't know it was for her. He was hired by a middle man. It was just a job."

It was Claire's turn to be bewildered. "How you know all that?"

"He told me."

"Who told you?"

"Ace. The boyfriend."

"But I thought—"

So he related his adventures of the night before. At the close of the recitation, she said, "With a Dustbuster?"

"What can I say? It's what we had handy."

There was a pause. The sun shone down. The waves hissed softly as they vanished. Here and there along the beach, people hit balls with paddles or chucked around a soggy football. Claire started doodling in the sand with a fingertip. She seemed to be working out some sort of diagram but it was unclear what it illustrated. "Okay," she said at last, "let's think this through. As of yesterday, you thought the boyfriend took the script so he could hit Donna with the speedboat. As revenge for dumping him."

"Yes, that's what I thought. I don't think it anymore."

140

"But now it looks like whoever has the script was really going after Candace."

"Yes," Jake agreed, "that's how it looks. Assuming you're right about the scorpion."

"But the fact remains that Donna has also been hurt."

"True."

"So what's the connection between Donna getting run over and Candace getting stung?"

"I haven't got a fucking clue."

As if exhausted by the puzzle, or maybe just cozened by the lapping water and the sand that molded itself beneath his body, Jake let his eyes fall closed. Claire did the same. The moment seemed so easy that the intimacy of it almost went unnoticed: two people, side by side, trusting to closed eyes and quiet in each other's company.

It was a wonderful respite but it couldn't last. There were too many questions tugging at the edges of it as at the corners of a quilt. Lifting his head, plunging, in spite of himself, back into the fray, Jake began, "So if the sister planted the scorpion, presumably she has a boat."

"Presumably," said Claire.

"And if she has a boat, she might also have been the one to run over Donna."

"But why would she? Her grudge is with Candace."

"Exactly. And Donna was doubling for Candace when she got hit."

"True. But this person has a script and schedule. The schedule lists the personnel for every shot. I mean, it's certainly possible that it was just a dumb mistake—"

"Or maybe not a mistake," Jake put in. "Maybe something else. A warning. A threat."

"Or a tease," Claire said. "This woman seems to like to tease."

Jake's scalp felt tight from thinking. He rubbed his head. As a bit of an afterthought, he said, "So how's she doing? Candace, I mean."

"Oh, she's fine. Those stings apparently hurt like hell but aren't really dangerous. She fainted, but only from the shock. I cleaned it out with ammonia, gave her some antihistamines. She'll be fine."

Jake said, "First aid is your job too?"

"Everything's my job. I'm getting really sick of it."

"Does she know about the paper you found? The page from the script."

Claire shook her head. "I didn't tell her. I didn't tell anyone. What would be the point? She'd be even more scared and the publicity people would have more grist for their bullshit story about the diva being targeted."

"Except," said Jake, "now it sounds like she really is."

In a tone more bemused than bitter, Claire said, "Whaddya know. Life imitates spin. Welcome to the entertainment business. On another subject, your shoulders are getting really red. Did you put sunblock on?"

"I forgot," he admitted. As an experiment, he poked a finger into the flesh at the top of his arm. The skin went dead white for a moment then flushed a hot angry orange-pink.

Claire reached into her bag and came out with a plastic bottle that she dangled in front of him. There followed one of those unemphatic but decisive moments that generally go unrecorded in a life, moments when some tiny gesture or lack thereof divides time into before and after and changes the trajectory of much that follows. Jake didn't take the bottle. He bided his time. He waited. And after a breath or two Claire squirted sunblock into her own hand and prepared to rub it onto his skin.

He pancaked flat against the sand, closed his eyes, exhaled, and opened himself to the pleasure of her touch. She anointed his neck and shoulders. Her fingers lightly kneaded the tops of his arms and then the palm of her hand bumped notch by notch over the vertebrae of his lean back. At times her touch was so light that he imagined he could feel the tiny whorls and ridges of her fingerprints; now and then he felt the hard tips of her nails just barely scratching at his flesh, holding the faraway promise of a tighter clasp sometime. He lay as still and quiet as he could, not wanting the luxury to end. When it finally did, he craned his neck around to smile at the woman kneeling over him. "This is starting to feel a little like a date," he said.

"Maybe just a little," she admitted. But then, jarringly, she added, "I think we need to find that crazy sister."

35

Meanwhile, at the compound that day, all was peace and domesticity. The pool pump softly hummed; birds chirped and warbled. Bryce in his phlegmatic way was trimming shrubbery. Now and then he actually made a snip with the shears; the rest of the time he just stood there and admired the mysterious spiral patterns by which the leaves and fronds unfolded.

Joey stopped by, together with Bert and the misnamed chihuahua, and was pleased to find Donna safe and reasonably sound, sitting in an umbrella-shaded lounge chair near the hot tub. He asked how she was feeling.

"Like the fucking Queen of England," she said. "Ace is taking care of me."

Behind the blue-lensed sunglasses, Joey could not help flinching.

Bert, seeming a bit confused, said, "Ace? Isn't that the guy we thought was gonna kill you yesterday?"

"It's fine," said Donna. "He loves me. He admits it now."

When Joey's face stayed skeptical, Donna gestured toward her feet.

"You don't believe it? Look at my toenails. Bert, check out those goddamn cuticles. Gorgeous, right? He gave me a pedicure. I told him I was depressed about my toenails. They looked like shit and I couldn't bend over to do them. So he did my toenails for me. On his hands and knees. I think that says something about the man. Don't you?"

Just then the gate swung open and Ace stepped through, his massive body largely hidden by two swelling bags of groceries.

Celery leaves and beet greens and carrot tops poked out of the sacks, reaching right up to his nose.

"Now he's gonna make me juice," whispered Donna, with just a hint of smugness. "Aren't you, honey?" she said in a voice that wafted sweetly across the gravel path. "Aren't you gonna make me some nice veggie juice?"

"Anything you say, baby. Anything to get you all fixed up."

He walked over and said a surprisingly cordial hello to Joey. With some effort, Joey managed to respond more or less in kind. Then he introduced Bert. Ace heard the name, saw what the old man was wearing—a peach-colored silk pullover with parrot-green placket, sleeve trim, and monogram—and did a double-take, the way one does when walking down an ordinary street and seeing a celebrity. He said, "Bert? As in Bert the Shirt? Bert d'Ambrosia?"

"The same."

"Hey, I hearda you."

Bert looked down, almost shyly, but he beamed. As a young man it had been so important to him to be taken seriously. Then for a brief time he'd wanted to be feared. Now, as an old man, all he asked or hoped for was to be a little bit remembered.

"You're like a legend," Ace went on. "The guy who was allowed to retire from the Mob."

Petting his dog, Bert said modestly, "I got out on a technicality. I died."

"Died?"

"Heart attack. Courthouse steps. Ambulance. Flat-line onna graph. I figured I fulfilled my oath: Come in living, go out dead."

Admiringly, wistfully, Ace said, "But you got out. That's the main thing. Hey, I'd really like to talk with you. Can you stick around a while? I gotta put these groceries away. Anybody want some veggie juice?"

Jacqueline Mayfield, the whirlwind publicist, had been summoned back to L.A. on an early morning flight. As instructed, she went straight to Quentin's office from the airport, and she found him looking awful. His complexion was sallow. There seemed to be more hints of gray hair on his temples than there'd been just a few days before. Behind his tint-shifting glasses, his eyes sagged slightly downward toward liver-colored sacs. Before he even said hello he said, "It isn't working."

"What isn't working?"

"None of it. Come in and close the door."

She stepped into the office. It was very L.A., large and bright yet still managing to be cheerless, sterile. White walls, glass shelves, two big windows overlooking Wilshire Boulevard. But there were no personal effects, no family photos, no goofy souvenirs. It was a lair beyond the reach of sentiment; it offered no clues about the person who worked in it and it killed nostalgia in advance. If a shift in fortunes were to sweep the current occupant from the privileged space, the walls would bear no memory that he had ever been there.

Jacqueline had barely settled into a chrome and leather chair when the producer went on. "The whole publicity angle," he pronounced, "has been a failure."

The publicist took this personally of course but saw no advantage in letting it show. Calmly, she said, "I thought it was going pretty well."

"Very well," he said, "if you were working for Candace McBride. But you're not. You work for me."

Jacqueline didn't like his tone at all. "I work for the show. You came up with this approach. I did everything I was asked to do to launch it, and more."

Quentin didn't disagree but he didn't give ground either. He gestured toward the stack of ratings reports and media clippings on his desk. "And this is the result. Candace is quickly becoming a household name and our numbers are going backwards."

"Backwards? Come on, it was a tiny bit of an off week. There's probably a lot of other factors–"

The producer didn't want to hear about the other factors. "Flops," he said, "are made of just slightly off weeks strung together.

I'm not going to sit here and wait for that to happen. We're reversing course."

"Reversing course?"

"We're pulling the plug on all publicity involving Candace. No interviews, no appearances, no nothing."

"Quentin, wait a second. I've got like six more spots already lined up."

"Cancel them."

"I can't cancel them. The shows are scheduled. The magazines are holding space. People will be furious."

"Good. Blame Candace. Say she cancelled everything. Say she's just too difficult. Make her poison."

Jacqueline folded her big hands in her big lap and took a moment to stare out the window. She searched for temperate words but then said what she thought. "That'd be a really pricky thing to do."

"Pricky? No. Practical. We built her up, we can bring her back to size."

"But why? I think you're making way too much of this one little blip. Can we please slow down a second? Can we talk it over?"

"No."

"Have you run it by the suits, at least?"

Quentin had laid his hands flat on his desk and he now leaned over them and pressed as if doing some peculiar sort of pushup. Sinews stood out in his neck and the skin went white at the edges of his eyes. When he spoke again his voice was thin and shrill. "I don't need to run it by the suits! You don't talk to the suits when the numbers are bad."

"They aren't bad," Jacqueline quietly insisted. "They're just a little—"

"They're bad!" Quentin yelled, slapping his desk and making pens and papers jump as he said so. The outburst left a queasy silence in its wake.

Very softly, Jacqueline said, "Are you all right?"

It was meant as a kindness but to the producer it seemed an intrusion and an affront. He shot his publicist an acidic glance. "I'm fine," he said. "I'm running a show. I'm taking care of business. There's a lot you just don't understand."

"Apparently."

The simple dry remark seemed to mollify him somewhat.

"Listen," he said, "this is an ensemble show. It doesn't work to have someone break out of the pack the way she has."

Finally unable to contain her exasperation, Jacqueline swelled in her chair and said, "Then why'd I work my ass off to make that happen?"

Scrambling now, as he did when cornered, Quentin said, "It was…let's call it an interim strategy. But it's over now. It's changing. We're going to be playing off of it, giving it a twist."

"A twist?"

"The Lulu character will be getting less important."

"Less important? And when did this get decided?"

The producer didn't answer, since it hadn't really been decided until he said it.

"Less important?" the publicist said again. "After the way we've put her front and center? That makes no sense."

"Oh but it does," said Dole, picking up momentum. "It makes perfect sense. It brings the focus back to the group. To the show itself. Don't you see?"

There was a pause. Quentin reached quickly for a pen, grabbed a random piece of paper and excitedly began to scribble down notes.

More animated now, he went on, "From here on in she recedes, she shrinks. There's a lesson in it, part of the mythology. She put herself before the group, and there are consequences. Serious consequences. Maybe…maybe she even has to die."

"Die? You'd kill off the most popular character? You'd write her out of the show?"

The producer no longer seemed to be listening. His head was down, his glasses were glinting light and dark, and he just kept scrawling notes. Jacqueline watched him for a while then slipped out of the office. He didn't seem to notice that she'd left.

36

Claire's luxurious rubbing of sunblock into Jake's neck and back and shoulders had given rise to some lovely daydreams full of promise but had come too late to spare him from a sunburn. By the time he got back to the compound, his skin felt papery, he itched around his hairline, and he had owlish pale circles where his sunglasses had been.

On a mission, he rolled the purple bike into its accustomed slot and went straight over to Donna's cottage, where he discovered a somewhat improbable tableau. Donna was sprawled out on the sofa, regally propped on pillows, sipping something green through a straw. She had a chihuahua on her lap, its chin and paws propped on her thigh. Bert the Shirt was relaxing in a love seat next to her, taking little nips of the same green liquid and trying to look happy about it. Ace was in the kitchen. He was wearing a pink apron printed with a pattern of little blue pots and pans that seemed to be floating gently through space. The apron covered only a narrow swath of his torso and its strings barely stretched around his back. He was deeply involved in an elaborate process of breading fish fillets, first bathing them in egg, then dredging them in flour, then egg again, then bread crumbs.

After a round of greetings, Jake said, "Sorry to barge in like this, but Ace, we have to talk."

Before Ace could answer, Donna said, "Would you like some veggie juice?"

"No. No thank you."

Ace said, "How about a beer?"

"Sure. Yeah. That'd be great."

Nodding toward the fridge, the big man said, "Help yourself. I'm all covered with egg and shit."

Jake grabbed a beer. "Thanks. But listen, there's something we have to–"

"Want to stay for dinner?" Donna asked. "Ace is really a good cook. We were just talking about that, saying that's what he should do from now on. Cook. Be a chef. Bert thinks it's a good idea. Don't you, Bert?"

"Lotta tough guys cook good."

"Ace's Place," Donna said. "Good name, right? Can't you just see it, Jake?"

Absently, Jake said, "Yeah. Great idea. But the reason I came over—"

"Try some grouper. You'll see how good it is."

"The reason I came over is that I need to know who hired Ace to grab that script."

Donna groaned and shifted on her pillows. "Oh Christ, this is where I was afraid you were going. This again?"

"Yeah, this again."

Ace dangled a fillet above a frying pan then gently swung it so that it made a perfect entry into the bubbling butter. Within seconds a heady fragrance filled the cottage.

Still trying to deflect, Donna said, "He puts nutmeg in the breadcrumbs. That's the secret."

"Fascinating. But about the script—"

Patiently, Ace said, "I thought we been through this. I don't think it's a good idea I tell ya."

"Maybe it's a good idea, maybe it isn't. But it's important."

Ace didn't ruffle. It was Donna who got exasperated. "For fuck's sake, Jake, everything's fine now. Why are you still—"

"Because everything isn't fine. Look, no offense, but I used to think Ace was the bad guy here. If he was, this would have been a pretty simple story. But he isn't. So the story turns out way more complicated."

"Story?" Donna said. "You think of all this as a story?"

Jake might have blushed but it was hard to tell through the sunburn. He felt a little caught, like the way he'd felt when Donna had seen him watching her swim naked. He said, "Sorry, I think of everything as a story. It's just my way. My way of trying to make sense of things."

Donna seemed to accept that. Ace, starting in on a second batch of fish fillets, said nothing. Bert took the opportunity to stop pretending he was drinking the veggie juice and to put the glass down on a table.

Jake sipped some beer and went on. "Look, weird stuff's been going on. Accidents that probably weren't accidents. You with the boat. Now Candace has been stung by a scorpion."

The stuntwoman, accustomed to the workday hazards of scrapes and sprains and broken bones, didn't seem particularly impressed. "Shit happens. Scorpions aren't exactly rare down here."

"Except this one was planted. Know how I know? Someone left behind a marked-up page from the script. *Your* script, I'm guessing. It looks like someone's out to torture her. Drive her nuts. Hurt her worse. Who knows?"

Fish sizzled softly in the pan. Ace, vigilant in his work, took small light-footed steps, boxer's steps, in front of the stove.

Donna said, "Candace getting tortured. I probably should be happy but I'm not."

Jake, misinterpreting, said, "Yeah, I think she's really shook."

"That isn't what I meant. I mean it's looking like that horseshit publicity angle is turning out to be true. Like it's been all about that prissy bitch right from the beginning."

"Maybe, maybe not," said Jake. "Look, the person who planted the scorpion must have had a boat. So it might be the same lunatic who ran you over. That's what I'm trying to figure out and why I need to find this person and figure out what her deal is."

Seeming to come out of a light stupor or momentary nap, Bert suddenly said, "Her? Did you say her?"

"Right," said Jake. "The sister of Candace's old boyfriend from L.A. Who killed himself when she dumped him."

"Sister," Bert murmured. "Family vendetta. That's not good. The brother—you say he's dead?"

"People who kill themselves generally are."

"That's not good," Bert said again. "Family shit, it's never really over. My guess, she'll end up icing her. Or trying, at least."

The mention of icing dug a deep trough in the conversation. It was Donna who dared to step across it first. She said to Jake, "Listen, I think you're making way too much of this. I got in the way of a boat. Candace got bit by a spider. Now you're making it sound like some big murder revenge thing."

"I'm not making it anything. It's there. Right in front of us."

"You have an active imagination, Jake. It's part of your charm. But wherever you're going with this, leave Ace out of it. He's finished with those people. He's gonna be a chef. Whatever happens from here, it has nothing to do with him."

Trying not to scratch his sunburn, Jake searched for a response but found none. None turned out to be needed.

Silently, resignedly, without fanfare, Ace had started taking off his apron. He labored with his bulky arms to untie the strings then coaxed the dainty pastel garment up over his leonine head. He said, "Sorry, baby, but it has a lot to do with me."

"No it doesn't," she shot back.

"Yes it does," he quietly insisted. "Stupid me is the guy that grabbed the script in the first place. What if what happened to you was my fault? I couldn't live with that. Or what if this Candace broad gets whacked?"

"Let her. I don't give a rat's ass about that."

"You don't mean that, baby. Maybe you wish you meant it, but you don't." To Jake, he said, "Tell me what you need to know."

Jake said, "The woman who bought the script. I need to know how to find her. That's all."

Ace nodded, looked wistfully at the perfect fish fillets he wouldn't get to eat, and felt in his pockets for his car keys. He walked into the living room and kissed Donna gently on the forehead. Then he asked his new idol, Bert the Shirt, the gangster who got out and lived to tell about it, if he felt like taking a ride.

37

Feeling like a kid brother who gets left behind while the bigger boys go off on an adventure, Jake stayed a while at Donna's and ate some grouper. It was delicious.

An hour later, he was back in his cottage, feet up on the bed, watching the slow and mesmerizing motion of the ceiling fan, when his cell phone rang. It was Quentin Dole, sounding calm, collegial, even chummy. "How's it going in Key West?" he asked.

Keeping it simple, Jake said, "Oh, fine. Just fine."

"Staying out of the bars long enough to get much work done?"

With barely a shred of guilt, Jake glanced over at the small desk in the alcove where his laptop still sat in its case. It had not been switched on even for a moment; not even taken out for show. He hadn't written a word of the book he'd been hired to write, and over the past couple of days it had been dawning on him, not by conscious thought but by a quiet yet fundamental shift in attitude, that he probably never would. "It's moving right along," he said.

"Excellent. You going with that story line I mentioned, about the secret weapon test?"

"Yeah, yeah. That was inspired. Sets the whole thing up."

The whole time Jake was bullshitting he was gazing at the laptop as if it were a totem. He clearly understood that he was sinning big-time by omission. This wasn't just a matter of missing a dead-line. It was a matter of completely, intentionally punting on a job, tearing up a contract, leaving a publisher with nothing to publish. It would be a huge black mark against the previously ultra-reliable ghostwriter; it might even wreck his career altogether. He found the possibility less terrifying than bracing.

"Glad it's working for you," Quentin said. "Is Lulu in it?"

"Lulu?"

"Lulu. The character in the show."

"Um, not yet. Should she be?"

"No. Definitely not. That's partly why I'm calling."

"But I thought—"

"—she was the franchise? I thought so too. But things evolve. Story lines change. Interesting process, isn't it?"

"Very."

"Well, keep up the good work. I'll be down your way in a day or two. We'll have a schmooze. Maybe you'll show me some pages."

Pages? The word caught Jake up short. Fumbling, stalling, he said, "You're coming here? Key West?"

"Mostly finished with a new script," Quentin said. "Very exciting. Bit of a bombshell, actually. The minute it's done I'm hopping a plane. Want to present it in person."

Hoping to keep the conversation far away from his non-existent pages, Jake said, "What's it about? Can you tell me?"

"You'll find out," the producer said. "Believe me, you'll find out."

In the quiet and safety of her suite at The Nest, Candace McBride was soothing her frazzled nerves by watching an old movie and sipping the contents of several small bottles, first of vodka then of cognac, from the mini-bar. The searing pain in her back had by now diminished to a vague heat and a faint throb that seemed somehow outside her body. As far as she knew, what had happened was an accident. Still, it came on top of various other stresses and worries, and she would have much preferred it to happen to someone else— a stuntwoman, say, or some other more dispensable person on the set. Then again, the scene they'd been shooting was a sexy one, a half-naked close-up with pouty lips and flirtatious dialogue; the sort of scene their adolescent viewers loved, that made the girls feel dreamy and inflated the boys with lust. No one but herself could have played that scene; that much she was sure of. She told herself that in getting stung she had suffered for her art.

Her attention divided between her self-admiring thoughts, the movie, and the cognac, she reacted only slowly to the knock on the door. "Yes? Who is it?"

"Housekeeping. Would you like turn-down service this evening?"

She didn't want to be bothered with turn-down service and she said so.

"May I just bring in some fresh towels and some chocolate for you?"

The actress hesitated. She didn't need more towels. Had the offer been for towels alone she would have told the housekeeper to go away. The chocolate was a different story. Chocolate was hard to pass up. A bit of chocolate and one more tiny bottle of cognac would cap the evening nicely. "All right. Come in," she said.

The housekeeper entered. She wore a starched but shapeless dress of institutional blue and her hair was pinned up in a cap made of paper. Although she seemed extremely nearsighted in thick-lensed glasses, she moved quietly and efficiently, first gliding to the bathroom to deliver a pile of neatly folded towels, then moving deferentially, not too close, toward the bed where Candace lay, and leaving a gold-wrapped bonbon on the nightstand. She turned to go, saying a soft and respectful goodnight that the diva did not bother to answer. She'd barely looked up at the housekeeper. Why would she? Housekeepers were generic, interchangeable. Though if she'd paid just a little more attention she might have noticed one incongruous detail. Beneath the frumpy blue dress, the housekeeper was wearing gold sandals whose undulating straps wound up her legs like intertwining snakes.

The door closed, and Candace wasted little time before reaching for the chocolate. With fingertips made slightly clumsy by eagerness, she tugged at the overlapping edges of the wrapper, then popped the bonbon into her mouth, briefly closing her eyes to concentrate on the intoxicating richness of that first taste. When she opened them again she saw the writing on the inside of the wrapper. There was an inexpert but unmistakable drawing of a scorpion. Next to it was the caption: *Feeling better? Not for long.*

Candace jerked and stiffened as though she'd been injected with another dose of venom. Coughing, gagging, she spat out what was left of the thickly melting chocolate, tried to call back the portion that had already trickled down her throat. Spasmodically, she threw her legs over the edge of the bed and trundled, crouched and heaving, toward the toilet bowl to kneel and vomit.

Standing again, she rinsed her mouth and threw cold water on her haunted face. Unthinkingly, she reached for one of the newly brought towels to dry herself and when she unfolded it she found that the inner layers had been soaked in blood.

38

Dusk is a contemplative time, a time that calls forth confidences, and on the leisurely ride up the Keys Ace poured his heart out to Bert the Shirt. He no longer wanted to live the life that he'd been living. The violence done to Donna had finally made him understand the ugliness of violence. He didn't have the stomach for it anymore and he was ashamed of many things he'd done; cowardly things, as he saw them now, to people much weaker than himself. He wanted a very different future for him and Donna and he didn't know how to get there from his past. Did Bert have any advice for him?

The old man stroked the chihuahua as if he was rubbing his own chin. Then he said, "You made?"

"Nah. Just an associate. I'm only half-Italian. Cuban on my mother's side."

"That should make it easier," Bert said.

Ace brightened.

"Not that it's ever easy," the Shirt went on.

Ace slumped a little in his seat.

"I mean, it's not like ya just send in a form or somethin'. Ya gotta…how should I put it? Ya gotta walk outa the room and keep on walkin' no matter what people yell at your back. 'Cause there's gonna be people tryin' to pull ya back in. With insults. With offers. There's gonna be resentment, jealousy. Most important thing, don't leave any messes, nothing that people can come after ya about. Ya leavin' any messes?"

Ace licked his lips and thought it over. "Just this bullshit with the script. I think that's it."

"Good," said Bert, and he spread out his yellowish hand to tick off another item on a big-knuckled finger. "Next thing, don't think ya can leave while owing any favors. Y'owe one of these dickheads a favor, he'll find you at the ends of the earth. Y'owe any favors?"

Ace pondered as he drove. After a moment, he said, "Ponte. Just a little favor. He loaned me a speedboat."

Bert shook his head. His big nose went back and forth like he was taking easy warm-up swings with a bat. "Due respect, Ace, there's a mistake in there. With Ponte there are no little favors. At least not if you owe him. Y'owe him, period. Better find a way to pay him back."

Ace took that in with a certain solemnity and for a while they drove on in silence. They crossed over bridges and causeways with pelicans gliding both above and below the roadway. Water curled around wooden pilings, cascading into tiny whirlpools on the lee side of the flow.

At some point Ace came out with a laugh and said, "Hey, Bert, ya know something that impresses me? We been driving for like an hour and you haven't asked me where we're going."

Stroking the dog, tugging softly at its all but hairless tail, Bert said, "If ya wanted to tell me, ya'd tell me. Besides, I know where we're goin'."

"No way."

"Ten bucks says I do."

"You're on."

"Okay, here's what I'm thinkin'. You're mainly Ponte's guy, so this is someone you know through Ponte. But it ain't Ponte himself and it ain't someone close to Ponte's level, 'cause, no offense, stealing a notebook is kind of a diddlyshit job. So it's someone farther down the food chain. And since it's wrapped up with this television bullshit, it's someone who has or likes to think he has some connection to show business. Now here's the capper. Since stealing someone's notebook is basically a sneaky, chickenshit thing to do, and since this guy didn't even have the balls to grab it himself but hired you to do it, then I say we're dealing with a sneaky fuck who always gets other people to do the work. Therefore I say we're headed to Handsome Johnny's Crab Joint."

"Amazing," said Ace.

"Basic," said Bert.

"I guess you really don't like Johnny."

"No, I don't. He's a two-cent turd with a hundred dollar haircut. Now gimme my fuckin' ten bucks."

Ace started stretching in the driver's seat to reach into his pocket.

"Nah, just kiddin'," the old man said. "But now that we know the kind of scumbag we're dealing with, how ya gonna handle the meeting?"

Ace's lips moved but no words came out. His hands lifted from the steering wheel and he shrugged.

"Ya don't have a plan?" said Bert. "No offense, but this is a mistake. Y'always have to have a plan. Plan might go to hell, plan might fall apart, but y'always have to have one. So come on, let's make a plan."

39

Around nine pm, while Jake was going slightly cross-eyed from lying on his back and trying to stop the blurry motion of the hypnotically turning ceiling fan, his cell phone rang again. It was Claire and she got straight to the point. "The scorpion lady has made another attack," she said. "We should talk. Can you meet me for a drink?"

So he got back on the purple bike and pedaled off to the place she suggested, a beachside restaurant called Ciaobella. She was already there when he arrived and she'd ordered a bottle of Vermentino. It was sitting in a silver bucket, leaning at a jaunty angle, streaming little rivulets of condensation and looking beautiful. Claire, with her hair down and wearing a simple cotton shirt, seafoam green, open at the throat, looked beautiful as well, and Jake dimly reflected that when you really liked a woman she got prettier and prettier every time you saw her. He felt an impulse to kiss her on the neck as he was moving around the table to sit down but he didn't do it.

He settled into his chair and a waiter poured the wine. The table was candlelit, with the classic red-checked cloth. Palms swayed all around them and twinkling stars were reflected in a faintly phosphorescent ocean. But while the setting was romantic, the conversation was rather less so.

"So she threw up the chocolate," Claire was saying, "and threw the bloody towels on the floor, then she called the front desk screaming hysterically, and the front desk called me, and we found the real housekeeper, who confessed immediately."

"Confessed to what?"

"To how the crazy sister got the uniform and the pass key. She slipped the housekeeper a couple hundred bucks and made it all sound like fun and games. A sex game, specifically. Hotel guest and maid. She said her boyfriend had always wanted to play that game, the thought of it drove him wild. She said the boyfriend was a guy on the show whose suite was next to Candace's. And the woman looked respectable and wealthy, so the housekeeper took the money and went along. Anyway, she's been fired and Candace is back in her room pumped full of Xanax with a security guard in front of her door."

Jake said, "And the chocolate?"

"What about it?"

"Was it poisoned?"

"Didn't seem to be. No ill effects. I think it was just a bluff, and a waste of perfectly good chocolate."

Jake drank some wine. Almost admiringly, he said, "Creative, this wacko sister. Resourceful. I kind of look forward to meeting her."

"Preferably," said Claire, "before our diva flips out altogether."

"It'll be soon," he said with more confidence than he felt. "Ace is on his way to try to find out where's staying, how to track her down."

Claire seemed relieved at that, but not very. "Good. That'd be good. Then what?"

Jake raised a finger as though to make a point but realized he didn't know what point to make. *Then what?* It was a question that had come up with relentless frequency these past few days and he never seemed to have an answer for it.

"I mean," Claire went on, "do we just go up and politely ask her to stop what she's been doing? And really, what *has* she done? We can't prove she planted the scorpion. Do they arrest people for impersonating a housekeeper? I mean, what do we really have?"

Jake pondered that, drummed fingers on the table. "My mind keeps skipping back to what happened to Donna. We know it wasn't

Ace. We know the sister's crazy. We know she has a boat. If only there was some connection—"

"That would be convenient," Claire cut in. "But isn't it possible that what happened to Donna and what's been happening to Candace are completely separate things, just parallel events? Maybe the connection is this: that there isn't one."

Jake was wearing a rather baggy linen shirt. The shirt had a droopy chest pocket into which he now reached, coming up with a small cheap notebook and a pen. He took a moment to scrawl something down.

Claire said, "You're taking notes?"

He said, "The connection is that there isn't one. That's pretty good."

She said, "You didn't take notes when you came down to the set."

He flipped the notebook closed and slipped it back into his pocket. "No, I didn't. What of it?"

Ace and Bert and the chihuahua strolled right past the No Dogs Allowed sign at the rather grandiose front entrance of Handsome Johnny's Crab Joint. Inside, the place was loud with the scraping of cutlery and the cracking of shells. The early birds had long gone home to doze in front of television; now it was the fancier crowd that filled the tables—lawyers down from New York for a few days' fishing, glistening Miami bigshots in linen and leather with their overdressed trophy wives or girlfriends.

Half a dozen people were lined up in front of the *maitre d*'s podium, which was arm's length from a giant tank full of crabs and lobsters. Ace, with Bert trailing in his wake, bulled right past the others to the front of the queue. This was part of the plan Bert had proposed.

Ace had been against it. "I don't wanna be pushy and obnoxious no more," he'd said. "I just wanna talk to the guy."

"Which will get you nowhere," Bert had said. "Look, the guy's a little pissant bully. But here's a secret. There's no one easier to bully than a bully. Ya just gotta bully him before he bullies you. So act mad, like you could blow at any second."

"But I'm not mad," Ace had said. "I'm back with Donna, everything's good. I'm not mad."

"I didn't say *be* mad," Bert had pointed out. "I said act mad. Fake it. It's a fuckin' game, man. You can do that, right?"

Ace wasn't sure if he could or not.

The first test came when the *maitre d'* looked up at him and said frostily, "Excuse me, sir, there are other people ahead of—"

Ace screwed down his features and cut him off. "I need to see Johnny."

The *maitre d'* didn't answer right away. Instead, he looked at the chihuahua that was dangling rather limply from Bert's crinkled hand. "And there are no dogs allowed in the restaurant."

Bert said, "This is a whaddyacallit, a service dog."

The *maitre d'* looked skeptically at the tiny animal. "I strongly doubt that, sir."

"You calling my friend a liar?" Ace said. "Get me Johnny. Now."

The *maitre d'* glanced briefly over his shoulder to a distant table where Johnny Burke, all smiles and pats on the back, was schmoozing with a prosperous-looking party of eight. "I'm sorry, but that's imposs—"

With a quick and compact motion Ace reached out and grabbed the other man's wrist, the one on which he wore his watch. His expression never changing, he squeezed. The *maitre d'* felt the hard edge of the casing bite into his flesh and had a moment to wonder which would give way first, the watch crystal or the small bones of his carpal tunnel. Ace said, "Get him." He waited for a small nod of assent before letting up the pressure.

In a few moments Johnny appeared. He and Ace stared at each other, their respective fake expressions a remarkable contrast. Johnny was furious but still wearing his unwavering public smile. Ace was actually quite calm but endeavoring to look like he might explode in the next heartbeat. In a hard whisper that didn't match his face, Johnny said, "What the hell you doing here?"

SHOT ON LOCATION

"Have to talk."

"At dinner hour? You just show up? I haven't got time."

"Make time."

"Look, I got a full place here—"

Johnny suddenly broke off, his eyes following Ace's to the lobster tank. Ace was almost having fun now, savoring the game, realizing that all it took was a glance to suggest he was crazy enough to lift the thing and tip it over, sending a tsunami of panicked crustaceans coursing through the restaurant. "All the more reason," he said, "not to make a scene, to keep things nice and quiet."

Handsome Johnny didn't answer that, just wheeled and led the way through the bustling dining room toward his office. He waved to everyone as he walked along and the show business smile never left his face and never varied.

40

At Ciaobella, the Vermentino was almost gone but neither Jake nor Claire was quite ready to have their time together end. They nursed their last half-glasses. Conversation came in scraps, sometimes comfortable, sometimes a little awkward. At some point Claire said, "Are you hungry at all? I feel like something sweet. They do an amazing *tiramisu* here. With mango slices."

"Share one?" he suggested.

This turned out to be a significant suggestion, because while they were sitting there at the candlelit table with palms swaying and the stars and ocean twinkling, a tiny but galvanizing event took place. They reached into the dessert at the exact same moment. Their forks touched, the ping of the small collision muffled by the rich texture of the cream. For just an instant the tines of their implements intertwined and locked. Fleeting though it was, it was a vicarious embrace, and not entirely a gentle one, fueled as it was by shared appetite, acknowledged hunger. Jake and Claire both felt the electricity of the proxy touch travel through their hands and up their arms. They pulled back quickly but a hint of titillation remained, as did a certain embarrassment, as if they'd been caught checking each other out across a crowded party.

Covering up, Claire said, "This is delicious."

"Really good," said Jake. He ate a morsel then put down his fork and dabbed his lips on a napkin.

"Not having any more?"

"No, just wanted a taste."

Claire took another bite. "Are you always so…so self-controlled?"

"No," said Jake, "I'm usually a seething cauldron of untamed cravings."

"Come on, I'm being serious. I want to know you better."

"Ah, so it's not about the *tiramisu* anymore?"

She moved some crumbs around on the plate. "Maybe, maybe not. But I was wondering if you've noticed that every time we've gotten together, I've called you. You've never called me. Not that I'm keeping score or anything. But are you always so...what's the word? Elusive doesn't quite describe it. Blase, but that doesn't really nail it either. Just sort of—"

"Chicken?"

"Not sure I'd say that."

"I would. Chicken. When I really like someone, I'm sort of chicken."

Claire was savoring one last bite of the sensuous dessert. "Should I take that as a compliment?"

"Absolutely."

Her eyes seemed to go a shade greener at that. She interlaced her fingers so they lay there in a cozy bundle. "What's to be chicken about? Me?"

"Not you. Not at all. Me."

"Okay, you. Want to tell me about it? I'll buy you a *grappa*."

While she was signaling for the waiter, Jake said, "I'll take the drink, but I'm not sure my story's worth the money. It's really pretty standard. I'm afraid I'll let you down."

"Let me down from what? We're pretty much at sea level now, right?"

"Right. But if we ever aren't...Look, this is just old stuff of mine. Not your problem at all."

"It's my problem if I like you," Claire said. "Besides, I've got a round of drinks invested here. So tell me."

Jake considered his *grappa* then took a small fiery swig. "Well," he said, "I was married for a while."

"Shocking revelation," Claire teased.

"And the marriage, in my mind at least, had a lot to do with my being an earnest young writer, a novelist. There was a romance to it. A purity. Does that make any sense? My wife was an editor, passionate about books. She understood what I was trying to do. So for a while the pieces just fit together. I was committed to my work. I was committed to the marriage. And I loved being committed. I knew who I was, I was happy with the choices I'd made. Then it all went south. The work didn't go so well, lots of rejection, and after a while my commitment to it had all been hammered out of me. I wish I could say I battled for years and years to be a real writer, but I didn't. I found I had this ghosting knack, so I took the path of least resistance and ended up with a career instead. But the purity was gone, the romance was gone. And the good parts of the marriage were gone too. I couldn't quite figure out how to be committed to something if I wasn't committed to everything. Anyway, I ended up being a big disappointment to my wife."

"She told you that?" Claire asked.

"She didn't have to. I felt it. And I resented her for making me feel it. Even though I knew, sort of, that it wasn't anything she was making me feel, it was something I was doing to myself. Which only made me feel worse, of course…And that's a long answer to why I'm afraid of getting together with a woman I really like."

He lifted his little *grappa* glass and they clinked. It was an odd statement to be toasting, but at least it was the truth. They looked at each other for a long moment. Though Jake didn't quite grasp this at the time, he was searching Claire's face for signs that she was giving up on him, writing him off after what she'd heard: being disappointed in advance. When those signs did not appear, he managed a smile and said, "Okay, now you show me yours. You're beautiful, smart, accomplished. And, as far as I can tell, single. How come?"

She glanced off toward the ocean and her eyes went briefly out of focus. "Actually," she said, "when I came down here and started working on the show, I wasn't single. Or at least I didn't think I was. I thought I had a boyfriend back in Santa Monica. But for some strange reason I didn't miss him. And the longer I was here, I missed him even less."

"Not a great sign," said Jake.

"No, but an interesting one. Because it made me wonder what kind of half-hearted relationship it had been in the first place if I could basically forget about it just because I had a job somewhere else. That seemed really kind of sad. It wasn't the guy's fault. He was nice enough. It was my fault. I'd been kidding myself that I had room for a relationship. But I didn't. I was too wrapped up in my work. Dealing with stuff 24/7, catering to everybody's feelings except my own. So I let the half-assed relationship go, and of course what happened then is that work started seeming even more important, to fill the void. Occasionally, during the rare moments when I could actually think and breathe, I'd ask myself why I was doing this, what I really wanted from it. Driving myself crazy with this job just so I'd get hired for the *next* job? So I'd be successful and exhausted and alone for a few more years? Or forever? What was the point? Then all this weird stuff started happening with Donna getting hurt and people playing creepy games with the publicity, and it all seemed pretty ugly. And just in the midst of that you showed up, and I actually was surprised to remember that not everyone in the world is a creature of the entertainment business, and now I'm in a complete muddle, no idea what I want or what I'm doing, and that's why I'm still single."

Jake said, "Wow, that's a lot of information for one glass of *grappa.*"

"Yeah, I guess it is. You asked for it."

"You asked for it first."

"Yeah, I did," said Claire. "And I'm glad. Aren't you?"

Jake had to think about it for a moment. "Yeah. I'm glad."

"And maybe just a little nervous?" Claire prompted.

"Yeah."

"I'm a little nervous too," said Claire. "But I think it's nice to be a little nervous, don't you? I mean, it's a nice change from not really caring one way or the other, don't you think?"

"Yeah," Jake said again. "I do think that. I think it's pretty nice."

41

Closing the door of his private office, Handsome Johnny also closed down the phony smile he no longer needed. He snarled, pulled his forehead into furrows, and said to Ace, "All right, you got five minutes. Fuck is this about?"

Only then did he seem to notice Bert and the chihuahua.

"And what the fuck are you doing here?" he added.

Bert said, "I'm his bodyguard. Thought he'd need one 'cause you're such a tough guy."

"Funny, Bert. Funny. And I guess your piece a shit mutt is a watchdog." He turned back to Ace. "Now you got four and a half minutes. Talk."

Uninvited, Ace had sat down on the edge of Johnny's desk. That was part of the plan as well: claim territory, crowd the space like a fighter cutting off the ring. He said, "That script you had me steal."

"What about it?"

"Ever since I brought it to you weird shit's been going on, people getting hurt."

Johnny shrugged. "Got nothing to do with me. I just passed it along."

"Who's the customer?"

"Privileged information," Johnny said. "You know I can't tell you that."

"Then I'll tell you," said Ace. "It's a crazy broad from L.A. whose brother killed himself and now she's raising hell."

Handsome Johnny flinched at that, just as Bert had predicted he would. It was often useful to surprise people with a piece of information they didn't know you had. It made them wonder how much else you knew. Trying to regain his equilibrium, Johnny said, "Okay, smart guy. Here's your gold star. Now what the hell you want from me?"

"You're gonna tell me how to find her."

At that Handsome Johnny smiled. It was a far different smile from the one he broadcast in the restaurant. This one was nasty, goading, provoking. His pissing contest smile. "And why would I do that?"

Ace leaned a few degrees closer to Johnny and squeezed the edge of the desk so that his knuckles changed color. He figured that would be enough. "I just have a feeling that you will."

"You threatening me, Ace?"

Ace said nothing.

Johnny said, "You know, all I gotta do, I tell Ponte I got a beef with you, and—"

"Ponte ain't here," Bert put in. "You guys are. I respectfully suggest youse work it out between the two a ya."

By that time Ace was leaning quite close to Handsome Johnny. Johnny, not wanting to give ground, was leaning gingerly toward Ace. Their chins were close enough together to smell each other's after-shave when Johnny decided that he was not in a promising posture. He backed off an inch or two and said, "All right, all right. Tell me why you got such a fucking hard-on about the script."

"My girlfriend got run over by a speedboat."

This news came as a complete and flabbergasting surprise to Handsome Johnny. Haltingly, he said, "Your girlfriend?"

"Donna Alvarez. The stuntwoman."

Johnny gave himself a quick beat to digest that. "Wait a second. You said you knew somebody on the show. You never said she was your girlfriend. You stole the script from your own girlfriend?"

Ace's tough-guy act frayed a little in that moment. A bit sheepishly, he said, "She wasn't my girlfriend then. We broke up. We're back together now. For good."

"Ah," said Johnny. He paced a couple of steps around the office while he tried to reappraise the situation. "So all this fucking drama, it's just a little personal matter?"

"Not so little. Very personal."

Sounding relieved and suddenly almost friendly, Johnny said, "Well, Christ, why didn't you say so? Personal I understand. Personal I respect. You want to track this nut-case down because she hurt your girlfriend, right?"

"If she did it. Yeah."

"And if she did, what then?"

Ace bunched up the muscles in his back and shoulders. His neck got so taut that his ears moved. That was answer enough.

Johnny said, "Okay. Okay. If that's how it is, I'll help you find her. But I want something in return."

"What a surprise," said Bert the Shirt.

Handsome Johnny let that pass. "This broad, I don't know where she is, but I know her boat and where she keeps it. But here's the deal. You find her, you do what you want. Get your satisfaction, I don't give a fuck. But the boat is mine. You grab it and bring it here. Okay?"

Johnny's face was stone but his heart was singing as he waited for an answer. He'd found a way, a perfect way, to turn this unwanted and unpromising meeting to advantage. As was his custom, he'd get somebody else—in this case, this lumpy moron Ace–to do some dirty work on his behalf. Then he, Johnny, would present the stolen boat to Charlie Ponte, who'd fence it for six figures, thereby repaying him for the bum loan to the suicidal director and getting Ponte off his back. It was perfect.

But then Ace said, "No dice. I'm not stealin' stuff no more."

There was a pause. Actually, there was some awkward fraction of a pause before Bert jumped in with one of his off-the-beat remarks. "Except maybe a speedboat now and then. A speedboat, he'll grab. Won't ya grab a speedboat, Ace?"

He read the old man's lifted eyebrow and said okay, he would.

Handsome Johnny smiled. "Good. The boat is at the Brigantine Marina, right in town. It's called the *Quickie*. Can't miss it. Iridescent blue-black, chrome pipes, custom everything. Grab the broad, grab the boat, everybody wins. Okay?"

Ace nodded, and Handsome Johnny, feeling like he'd got his way, like he'd outsmarted and outmaneuvered everybody, grew downright charming and affable. He offered cigars, which were declined. He looked kindly at Bert's chihuahua and said, "Mutt's actually kind of cute."

He reached out to pet the dog. The dog growled and tried to bite his finger.

"And an excellent judge of character," said Bert, as they headed for the door.

42

At five a.m. West Coast time, Jacqueline Mayfield was already wide awake. Drinking coffee, padding around her apartment in very large and very fuzzy slippers, she was bracing herself to make a phone call she'd been dreading. She sat down on a sofa, propped her feet on an ottoman, and speed-dialed Candace McBride to tell her that her morning interview with *TV Insider* had been cancelled.

Until she'd heard the word, Candace, still in bed, had been groggy from last night's booze and Xanax. Suddenly she wasn't. "Cancelled? What do you mean, cancelled?"

"They changed their minds. They don't want the segment."

"Changed their minds? They begged for this interview. They promised us the lead slot, asked for clips from the show…"

Gently but not quite apologetically, Jacqueline said, "What can I tell you? They wanted it. Now they don't. I can't see inside their heads."

The diva went silent for a moment. Even alone in her hotel bed she was acting. Her face ran through a number of expressions, from surprise to anger to resignation to a sort of droll rising above. "All right, all right," she said. "Guess I'll have to save the charm for the *Red Carpet* spot this evening."

The publicist swallowed some coffee. "Actually you won't. That one's off too."

"What?"

"It's off. The whole week's schedule is off. Sorry, but that's how it is."

Candace sat bolt upright in bed and swung her feet onto the floor. The quick movement made her head pound. She squinted past her drawn blinds and could just make out the silhouette of the security guard at her door. "How it *is*?" she hissed. "Jacqueline, what the fuck are you telling me?"

The big woman put her coffee down and indulged in an inaudible sigh. Like any good publicist she could bullshit with the best of them, but the easy flow of fibs and euphemisms and strategic exaggerations depended to a fair degree on a genuine enthusiasm for the message. The enthusiasm was in itself a kind of truth, if not the purest sort; but without it the stretches and evasions felt thick and dirty in her mouth and she just couldn't sell them. "Honey, listen, you're a lot more famous than you were a week ago. You've had the kind of exposure actors dream of. Enjoy that."

The star was up and pacing now. "Enjoy it? Enjoy it…like, it's over?"

The publicist said nothing.

"Why's it over, Jacqueline? Why's it suddenly over? Everyone cancels on the same day? That makes no sense to me. I don't believe it. They didn't cancel. You cancelled. Didn't you?"

"Candace—"

Crouching low, tugging at her hair, the actress said, "Just tell me the fucking truth. You cancelled my appearances, didn't you?"

Softly, evenly, Jacqueline said, "Yes. I did."

"You fucking bitch."

"It's a brutal business, Candace. The way decisions get made, it isn't always—"

"You fucking bitch," the diva said again, and broke off the connection.

Jacqueline Mayfield stared at her silent phone for just a moment, then finished her coffee and padded off to the shower to get ready for the rest of her day's work.

Jake was dreaming of bacon.

Gradually he realized that he wasn't dreaming, that someone was cooking breakfast on the communal gas grill right in front of his cottage. He got out of bed and peeked through a gap in the shutters to see Ace cracking eggs into a skillet. The eggs looked tiny in his enormous hands but he cracked them with finesse and tenderness, as if he hoped to put the shells together again after he had drained them.

Jake threw some water on his face and joined him on the patio. Ace asked him if he wanted some food. He waved the offer away. "Too early for me. How'd it go last night?"

Checking the doneness of the bacon with a pair of tongs, Ace said, "Went good. The crazy sister, I know the name of her boat. I know where she keeps it. Couldn't find it though."

"You went looking?"

"Me and Bert, we got back to town, it was pretty early yet, we figured we'd check out the marina. But it's gated on the land side. Couldn't see much. Couldn't get onto the docks. Need to scope it out in daylight. From the water side."

Jake nodded but he was still a little drowsy, a little fuzzy from the Vermentino and the *grappa,* and the nod referred to nothing in particular.

With a feathery touch Ace flipped a couple eggs, keeping the yolks perfectly intact. His eyes still on the skillet, he said, "Bert says Joey has a boat, a little fishing skiff. We'll take a cruise around a little later."

The *we* was vague and Jake wasn't quite sure if it meant he was invited. But he knew he didn't want to be left behind again. He said, "I want to go along."

Ace seemed surprised by the remark. "Of course you're going along. You're the one that's gotta tell us if that's the boat that almost killed Donna."

Quentin Dole had worked through the night, had worked with a relentless energy that banished fatigue and obliterated the usual sense of the passage of time. He was by nature a spasmodic writer, someone who might stare into space for twenty minutes then put his head down over the keyboard and type non-stop for an hour.

But with this script the rhythm was very different. The words flowed forth not in bursts but with a not quite human steadiness. There was something automatic, inexorable in the way that speech followed speech and scene followed scene. It was almost as if Dole was not creating the script but hearing it, not inventing but taking down dictation. When he'd finished the episode and held the printed pages in his hand, he didn't quite remember having written them. But he knew they were right; he knew they told the story of what had to happen next in the universe of *Adrift*.

He slept for a fitful hour before booking a flight to Miami. Then he called his newly found and newly solicitous father and asked or rather commanded him to meet him at the airport.

43

Joey Goldman's boat wasn't much to look at, just eighteen feet of bland and slightly dinged up fiberglass, some sun-faded blue seat cushions, and a well-worn outboard engine that usually but not always took him where he wanted to go. He kept the modest craft at Garrison Bight, the locals' marina, where teak was seldom oiled, brass was rarely buffed, and every once in a while a venerable houseboat or trawler would silently settle to the bottom of its slip, coming to rest at a picturesque angle in the fragrant mud.

Now Joey and his passengers pulled slowly away from the funky dock, and when they'd scudded under the Fleming Key bridge and through the upper harbor to round the breakwater that led to the privileged precinct of the Brigantine Marina, they looked like poor relations arriving for a strained, unwelcome visit, or maybe more like refugees pulling into some barely believable promised land. The tall raked masts of million dollar sloops and ketches towered over them. They were dwarfed by the gleaming tuna towers and pendant outriggers of rich men's occasional fishing boats.

Donna, her arm still in a sling but her color and sass largely restored, said, "No offense, Joey, but people'll think we're someone's dinghy."

"Let 'em think what they want," said Bert, who was dressed in red and white seersucker for the excursion. His dog had a tiny yellow life vest on. "Snob bastards."

At idle speed, Joey weaved through the mooring field and up and down the ranks of floating piers. Here and there, amid the sailboats and the cabin cruisers, speedboats were roped into their berths. There was something odd and rather sad about these speed-boats: In their overreaching attempts to be distinctive they all ended up, like society women in extravagant hats, looking more or less the same. Lots of chrome. Swollen phallic hulls. Rich and sinister finishes leavened with flecks and sparkles. Looking at these flashy vessels, Jake begged his eyes to discern details, telltale quirks, but he felt a secret fear of failure. He doubted he could tell one speedboat from another.

Then they found the *Quickie*. It was tied up between a big wooden yawl and a high-tech racing sloop. The name was painted in fancy gold script on a tapering transom. The pipes and windshield glared blindingly in the late morning sun. The dock lines were slack and the muscular hull sat perfectly still in the sheltered water. Joey eased to within five feet of its stern.

Ace said to Jake, "Zat it?"

Jake stared, thought, hoped that memory might trump imagination as he tried to picture truly what had happened on the morning of Donna's big swim. He saw again the speedboat appearing with horrible abruptness in the channel between the islets; he recalled the looming menace of the lifted hull; he remembered watching distance shrink between the boat and its victim then stretch again as the guilty craft sped remorselessly away. He stared at the *Quickie* for a few long moments, pursed his lips, then just shook his head.

"That isn't it?" said Ace.

Unhappily, Jake said, "I don't know. It might be. I'm just not sure."

Ace looked at Bert. Bert looked at Donna. Donna said, "Don't ask me, I was underneath the sonofabitch."

Joey idled for another moment. He was just clicking into reverse when a tall blonde woman in amber sunglasses appeared at the head of the dock, just outside the fence, perhaps a hundred feet away. She wore a chic leather jacket that was far too snug to close, but left a swath of cleavage and taut flat midriff exposed to the air and sunshine. On her feet were golden sandals whose straps wound up her calves.

She was punching in a gate code when she noticed the crummy little skiff that was loitering near her boat. She stopped what she was doing, watched, appraised. Sightseers? Gawkers? It took a moment before anyone in Joey's craft saw the woman standing there, and then everyone seemed to discover her at once. Heads turned, gazes locked in. The woman didn't budge, didn't flinch, didn't look away. As the seconds passed, her immobility seemed more and more a dare, a taunt.

Never taking his eyes off the blonde, Ace said in a rough whisper, "Put me ashore."

With one jerk of the motor Joey maneuvered toward the pier and the big man leaped onto it. Jake, by reflex, followed him, and the two of them, first jogging then sprinting, dodging coiled ropes and stacks of gear, labored up the floating dock that rocked and tilted under the pounding of their feet. For an instant more the blonde just looked at them, then she wheeled and moved away. She didn't panic, didn't run, just walked quickly with a confident and mocking step, a bag slung across her shoulder and bouncing on her hip.

At the head of the pier, Ace swung open the security gate and lumbered through it, Jake closely following. But as soon as the water and the boats were behind them, they found themselves without transition in a teeming bazaar of shops and kiosks, cafes and bars. Chairs and tables spilled across the sidewalk, almost to the shoreline; early drinkers sucked tall Bloody Marys through straws. Phalanxes of shoppers glutted up the passageways, lugging souvenirs, taking pictures. Ace and Jake peered left and right, ran a block in one direction, then, winded and sweating, doubled back the other way, sidling and dodging as they went. But there was no trace of the taunting blonde. Somehow, even with her unmistakable strangeness, she had melted into the milling crowd. She was as gone as though she'd never been there.

44

As usual, it was Claire who was expected to bear the brunt of Candace's unhappiness, this time brought about by the cancelling of her publicity appearances. During a break in that day's shooting, the diva came barging into her metal box of an office and said without prelude, "You've heard what that bitch Jacqueline did to me?"

Claire was elbow deep in mundane paperwork—union time cards, caterer's bills. Without looking up she said, "Yes, I've heard."

Redundantly, hoping to draw the other woman's gaze, Candace said, "Cancelled my interviews. Every one."

Claire kept working, her eyes down on her papers. "Yes, I've heard," she said again. She said it very calmly and without much apparent interest or sympathy. This confused and rattled Candace. Why wasn't Claire responding as she should, as she always had before? Why wasn't she swept at once into the drama?

Upping the ante, the actress put a hand on her hip and dipped her shoulders forward. With her free hand she loudly snapped a finger. "Just like that," she said. "No warning. No explanation. No gratitude for everything I've done."

Claire briefly put her pen down. "Gratitude? How about gratitude on your side?" She went back to the tasks in front of her.

"On my side?" said the diva, her voice rising in disbelief. "For what? Being kept up all hours of the day and night? Getting stung? Getting poisoned?"

"You weren't poisoned. It was chocolate. Look, you didn't have to go along with the publicity. You did it because you wanted the attention. You got it, and all you did was complain. Now you're losing it and you're complaining again. Which is it, Candace? Make up your mind."

The actress stared back at Claire for just a heartbeat, then she turned and strode the short length of the metal office, her forearm raised across her brow. Peering back over her shoulder she whimpered, "So you're against me too."

Wearily, softly, Claire said, "I'm not against you. And by the way, neither's Jacqueline. But speaking for myself, I'm sick and tired of babysitting you. You're a real pain in the ass, Candace."

The words could not have been much simpler but it seemed to take a while for the actress to process them. Behind her eyes she was riffling through her repertoire of possible reactions. Righteous outrage? Wounded feelings? Treating the comment as a bit of a joke? But nothing in her well-schooled range seemed to fit the naked truth of the moment and she stood there blankly, wondering what she ought to feel.

Instead it was Claire who finally let the emotions fly. Months of forbearance, of overwork, of acting on decisions she did not believe in and taking care of everyone except herself finally overwhelmed her tact, and she allowed herself the luxury of candor. "You're more trouble than the rest of the cast put together. You're selfish. You're oblivious. You're cruel to less important people. You're talented but you're a nightmare, Candace. Now if you'd please leave, I have work to do."

Claire's heart rate had returned to normal and she was unconsciously whistling when her cell phone rang. It was Jake.

"Know why I'm calling?" he asked.

"No idea."

"I'm calling because you say I never call and that I'm never the one to see if we can get together. So I'm calling not to be a chicken and to ask if I can see you later."

Claire was pleased enough that her peachy skin flushed beneath the suntan. "Well," she said. "You're the second person who's surprised me today."

"Who was the first?"

"Myself. I just told off Candace."

"Good for you."

"Maybe. Felt good in the moment. But, you know, it's partly your fault."

"My fault?"

"These last few days," she said, "hanging around with you, talking, I've finally been thinking about what I want for a change."

Jake said, "So that means we can get together?"

"Sorry, but actually we can't. Not today. Quentin's coming into town."

Impressed, Jake said, "Wow, he finished his script already? That's some fast writing."

"He got on a roll and worked through the night. Didn't even talk with the staff writers. Just powered through it. Sounded really wired when he called. Said he was catching an early flight."

"So he's in Florida already?"

Claire looked at her watch. "No, it'll be another hour or two. You know, with the time difference. But I've got a bunch of grunt work to do in the meantime. Can we get together maybe tomorrow?"

"Sure," Jake said. "Sure."

There was one of those dangling pauses that happen when a conversation is basically over but two people aren't quite ready to break off the tenuous intimacy of a phone call. Finally Claire said, "I gotta go. I'm really glad you called."

She tried to get back to her paperwork but had a little trouble concentrating. Two minutes later her cell phone rang again.

Before he even said hello, Jake said rather breathlessly, "The time difference."

He was calling from his cottage, which suddenly seemed too small to contain the excited circuits of his pacing. Leaning far forward, flapping his free hand in some emphatic yet vague explanatory gesture, he said again, "You said the time difference. It didn't register before."

Claire said, "I have no idea what you're talking about."

Knowing he was rambling, but too amped up to fix it, he said, "I just thought of this. Quentin's early morning flight. Early morning in California. Not here. Three hours later here. So by the time he gets to Florida it's late afternoon."

Patiently, Claire said, "Yes, the earth revolves. That's how time zones work. "

Cutting in again, Jake said, "Three hours later for the time change. Four, five hours for the flight."

"Right. So Quentin will be in Miami around four. I don't see–"

"Except I'm not talking about Quentin now."

"Excuse me?"

"I'm talking about Jacqueline. Jacqueline got here too soon."

Claire said, "Jake, I'm not really following this. Can you please slow down a little?"

He tried to. He plopped down on the sofa in his living room and pegged his elbows on his bony knees. "Okay. Okay. The day Donna got run over. She got hurt...when? Around ten. When did Jacqueline land in Miami? Around two, right? Isn't that when it was? Two p.m. East Coast time. Do the math. There weren't enough hours. She would've had to get the news, get to the airport. It should have been more like two o'clock *Los Angeles* time when she landed. More like five out here."

"So you're saying—"

"I'm saying she was on her way before Donna got run over." He paused and let the words sink down like mud to the bottom of a puddle. "Like maybe she knew it would happen."

Claire pondered but resisted. "Whoa, that's quite a stretch. Just because she happened to be on an early flight? Maybe she was coming anyway. For something else."

"Maybe she was. You tell me. What else would she have been coming for?"

"I...I don't know," said Claire. "But they don't tell me everything."

"They seem to tell you most things."

Still skeptical, still fending off belief, Claire stalled a moment then murmured, "But Jacqueline? I just can't imagine..."

"What? That she'd sacrifice a stunt girl for a terrific story? For a first-class publicity blitz that would look very glossy on her resume? It's the entertainment business, right?"

Claire searched for a response and in the meantime Jake sprang up, resumed his pacing, and let his hunch carry him still farther.

"Couldn't've been Jacqueline alone, of course. There needed to be someone else. Someone here. Someone with a speedboat. Maybe someone Jacqueline knew from before, from Los Angeles. Like maybe the crazy blonde."

"Now wait a second," Claire protested.

He didn't. "Think about it. Think about their two agendas. Jacqueline wants her story. The crazy blonde wants Candace front and center, out in the open, so she can get to her, torment her, bring her down. Donna gets hurt and they both get exactly what they want. Look, we've been trying to figure out a connection between what happened to Donna and what's been happening to Candace, right? Maybe this is the connection."

Claire, trying to follow the rush of Jake's hypothesizing, had been doodling some of her complex but obscure diagrams on random scraps of paper. "I don't know," she said, examining her arcs and triangles. "It just sounds a little, a little—"

"Show me the flaw in the logic," he challenged. "Show me where the logic doesn't wash."

"The logic seems fine," she conceded after another moment's thought. "Then again, it was pretty logical to think it was Ace. A little proof would be nice."

"One thing at a time," Jake said. "One thing at a time. I'll see you tomorrow."

45

"Just read it," Quentin Dole had said as he handed copies of his freshly-printed script to Claire and to Rob Stanton. "We'll talk about it after."

They were meeting in the producer's suite at the Flagler House hotel. As of when his visitors arrived, Dole had not even taken time to unpack his small travel bag. He hadn't taken time to shave that morning either. He'd caught a bit of sleep on the plane and his cream-colored silk shirt was rumpled. His skin sagged as though from a sudden weight loss on his already attenuated frame. The lenses of his glasses went darker and lighter, lighter and darker, as the sun moved in and out of clouds and burned at different angles through the half-drawn curtains of the sitting room. Once the scripts were handed out, he went into the bedroom and closed the door behind him.

There followed an extremely uncomfortable half hour for the director and the line producer. They sat diagonally across from one another, Stanton in a love seat, Claire nestled in a corner of a sofa. They read silently, now and then crossing or uncrossing their ankles, occasionally, surreptitiously, peeking up at one another, looking for clues about the other's reaction. When they'd read roughly half the pages, Quentin reappeared. His hair was wet and he was wearing an oversized and luxuriously fluffy terry-cloth robe. He didn't speak, didn't sit, just padded around the living room and watched his colleagues read. There was something about him in those moments—maybe the fur-like robe, maybe the silence of his footfalls in the terry slippers—that gave him the aspect of a watchful cat.

Claire and Stanton, attuned to the rhythm of television scripts—the clipped cadences, the fraught set-ups for commercial breaks--finished reading at nearly the same instant. They each put their copies on a coffee table between them; neither wanting to speak first, they both fussed with the pages, squaring them up just so.

Finally, Quentin Dole said, "So?"

The director and the line producer glanced at one another. Claire succeeded in waiting out Rob Stanton.

"It's brilliant," he said. "Brilliant. But—"

"But what?" said Dole, ahead of the beat, teeth a little bit bared, as if he was trying to bite off the objection while it was just a nub.

"But...it's pretty radical. Such a jolt."

"Exactly! A radical jolt is just what we need." Abruptly yet smoothly, the producer perched himself on the very edge of an armchair. "You know what's death to a show like this? Comfort. People want comfort, let them watch *Cheers* reruns. Nice, soft nostalgic comfort. That's not what we do. We do edgy. We let viewers relax, we're toast. What we need is shock. Unpredictability. That sense that no one's safe, anything can happen. Like it does in life."

"Except it isn't life," said Claire. "It's a television show. With things like viewer loyalty to consider. Loyalty to certain characters."

"Viewer loyalty? How quaint. Come on, Claire. A crap show with buzz comes into our time slot and viewer loyalty is out the window. You know that as well as I do."

Rob Stanton jumped back in, taking a different tack this time. "That scene," he said, gesturing toward the stack of pages on the coffee table. "The tragedy, the climax. I'm not sure it's even possible to prep for it without a bigger crew."

"We've got a bigger crew," the producer said.

"We do?"

"Construction guys. I hired some in Miami this afternoon."

"Way ahead of me as usual," Stanton conceded.

"And later on they'll be digging out a perfect imitation of a Florida sinkhole. The kind that open up all the time where water eats at coral. Perfectly believable. Perfectly shocking if someone were to vanish into it."

Claire said, "Quentin, are you really sure you want to do this?"

Without hesitation, he said, "Yes. And I want it shot tonight. Before there's any chance of spoilers leaking out."

"Tonight? But—"

"The cast will get their scripts at six. We'll prep the set at eight, take a break, start shooting the lead-in stuff at midnight. Candace comes on for her big scene right at sunrise."

More sharply than she meant to, Claire said, "That's a terrible idea. It'll be a mess. Everyone'll be exhausted."

"Precisely," Quentin said. "As people often are when a real disaster hits. Exhausted and raw, emotions stripped bare. Messy I don't mind. But I want it raw. I want it real. This is not open to discussion. That's the schedule."

There was a silence. Rob Stanton's fingers twitched as if he was already counting scenes, allotting crew and cameras. Quentin Dole finally let himself settle partway into his armchair. Very softly Claire said, "Who'll tell Candace?"

The producer seemed surprised by the question. "Tell her? What's the need to tell her? She'll find out when she reads the script."

Rising from her corner of the sofa, Claire said, "That's horrible, Quentin. That's really horrible. I'll go talk to her. See you at the set."

46

In her small but airy bedroom, in front of slanting Bahama shutters that sliced and softened the reddish light of late afternoon, Donna was doing some very slow and very careful stretches. It felt odd to her to be so cautious with the body she had always taken for granted and in fact been entirely fearless with. But now even the slightest flexings called for prudence, each movement demanded deliberation and restraint. If there was frustration in this forced heedfulness, there was tenderness as well—a tenderness for her physical self that she hadn't felt before. Knowing that she could be hurt, she cherished her bones and sinews and felt gratitude for the miracle of healing, this amazing ability for broken things to fix themselves.

She bent and leaned to the rhythm of measured breathing, and Ace was watching her the whole time, silently encouraging, his breaths unconsciously tracking hers. She was wearing a pale yellow slip. It clung to her breasts and hips but when she moved in certain ways the fabric fell away from her skin and light shone through it, dimly tracing arcs and hollows. She felt Ace's eyes and enjoyed the feeling.

At some point she said, "Honey, will you help me off with this thing?"

Ace's mouth went instantly dry. He'd been missing her badly. On tingling legs he crossed the small space between them and gently reached down toward the hem of her slip.

"No," she said. "I meant the sling. I want to try out my arm."

"Oh."

Reading his face, she said, "You thought I meant my slinky little undergarment? I'm so sorry. I didn't mean to tease."

Teasing back, Ace said, "I think maybe you did."

"Maybe just a little," she admitted, and she kissed him on the cheek. "We're gonna have amazing times, you know. Amazing."

"You're killin' me here," he said.

"Myself too. Come on, help me get this off."

He reached out and, with fingers that trembled slightly with thwarted desire, he undid the clasp that held the sling in place. The cloth fell away and he cupped her elbow in one giant palm, her wrist in the other. Slowly, carefully he lowered her hand to her side. At first the dangling arm did not seem to belong to her; it was just a weight that hung there. Then, not without surprise, she found that she could move it. Little by little she tested it out: elbow bent, elbow straight; fist clenched, fingers splayed; wincing now and then, she raised the damaged limb a little higher, a little higher, and every inch she raised it was a victory.

Seeing the effort that it cost her, Ace said, "Maybe that's enough for now."

For Donna it wasn't quite enough. She gritted her teeth and pushed for one more centimeter, then exhaled through pursed lips. "It's gonna be okay," she said. "I'm gonna get it back."

At Nellie's, Candace was sitting at the quiet bar, an unpeopled frontier of randomly swiveled stools on either side of her. Her head was tilted down in a sulk and her elbows were planted on either side of her glass of wine, held in close together as if defending against body blows. She barely looked up when Claire approached and said a cautious hello.

"Oh, hi," she answered without enthusiasm.

"May I sit a minute? I owe you an apology."

"No you don't."

"I was pretty harsh before."

Candace shrugged. "You didn't say anything that wasn't true. Have a glass of wine?"

Claire nodded and a bartender suavely appeared out of nowhere.

"I'm the one who should apologize," the diva went on. "To you. To everyone. I've been awful. I know it. And I can't stop. Why am I so awful?"

Soothingly, Claire said, "The show's been crazy. So much pressure."

Candace shook her head. "Thanks for the good excuse. And I could find others, I guess. But they're just excuses. The truth is that I've handled things badly. Everything."

Claire gestured as though to disagree but found that she couldn't.

"You know what it is?" the actress continued. "It's this fantasy I've had forever and now I'm stuck with. Being famous. Being a star. In the fantasy it's very simple, all one-sided. Never what I'd give, only what I'd get. Never what I'd owe anybody else, only what they'd owe me. Then the fantasy becomes reality, and all this other stuff—being nice, being gracious—is just a big fat fucking mystery. I've never practiced it. I don't know how to do it."

"Maybe just takes time," said Claire. "Time and feeling secure."

Candace drank some wine then gave a rough quick laugh and almost choked on it. "Feeling secure. That's a good one. Well, I'm going to work at it. Being nicer, I mean. Giving back. I've promised myself I will. I'll use my standing on the show—"

"Um, Candace, we need to talk about that."

The crazy blonde with the gladiator sandals had not seemed panicked by the boatload of gawkers who'd shown up at her marina, nor even by the mismatched pair of men who'd appeared to be pursuing her up the dock. True, she'd fled; but there had been a goading insouciance in how she did it. She didn't run. She'd never once looked back to track the progress of the chase. She merely walked away at a brisk though hardly desperate tempo, using the dockside bustle and brightly dressed crowd to hide her.

But for all her infuriating casualness, Marguerite Bouchard was deeply distressed to realize that people were finally on to her.

Her concern was not for herself—in the grip of her obsession she really didn't care if she was caught, arrested, put away–but for the success of her mission. She'd dreamed so fervently of avenging her brother; she'd plotted her campaign with passion and care. And what had she really accomplished so far? She'd caused her enemy some stabs of pain, some moments of paranoid anxiety. It wasn't nearly enough. There was much more to be done and she couldn't let herself be caught just yet, couldn't let herself run out of time.

One thing was clear. If people knew about her speedboat, she couldn't leave it just sitting where it was—not right downtown where anyone could find it. She needed to be moving now; she no longer had the luxury of staying still, watching and waiting. At sunset she returned to the Brigantine Marina. She scouted for snoops and gawkers then slipped aboard the *Quickie*. The engines roared and clattered to life and she plowed a deep wake through the harbor before heading south then east toward the open water and name-less islets of the Keys.

47

Jake was sitting poolside, savoring the small and valedictory pleasures of dusk—the sudden quiet of the birds, the soft and spinning fall, one by one, of that day's hibiscus blooms—when he recognized Claire's number on his silenced phone. Feeling for the moment blithe, playful and fleetingly confident, he picked it up and said, "Just can't stay away, huh?"

Claire was not in the mood for repartee. She said simply, "I need to see you. I'm really worried."

Nonplussed by her tone, Jake fumbled. "Well, sure. Where? When?"

"I'm heading to the set. Can I pick you up?"

Five minutes later he was standing in front of the compound gate when her limousine came crunching over the gravel. He slid in close to her but she seemed too agitated to be sociable, still less romantic. She got right down to business. "Lulu's getting killed tonight. Tomorrow at sunrise to be exact."

"What?"

"Lulu. Candace. She's being written out of the show. Quentin wrote her out."

"But—"

"His crazy script. He wants it shot tonight. All very rush-rush-hush-hush. It's weird."

Jake pondered that but before he could answer Claire went on.

"And of course I'm the one who had to tell Candace. She was right in the middle of one of her new leaf speeches. You know, how she's going to be a better person from now on. That went out the window as soon as she got the news. She's probably back in her room screaming at her agent, doing pills and vodka. I just hope she doesn't slur through her big sayonara scene."

The limo turned north on U.S. 1. The pastels and gingerbread of Old Town yielded to the jangly neon of the strip malls and motels.

Jake said, "But why the sayonara scene at all? Why kill her off after making her the center of the show?"

"An excellent question," said Claire. "One possibility is that Quentin's way smarter than any of us, way better at staying one step ahead of the fans. Another possibility is that he's totally flipping out."

Jake considered that but came away doubting it. "Seems a little too dramatic. I mean, he's obsessive, he's controlling—"

"Right. And where does obsessive and controlling cross over into loony?" The question hung for a moment, then Claire added, "I called the publicist."

"You what?"

"Jacqueline. I called her. I'm sorry but I had to. I've worked with her for months. It just didn't sit right that you were suspecting her."

"So you casually rang her up and asked if she'd conspired in any murder attempts lately?"

"I just asked her how she happened to be on that early flight. Just casually asked."

"And?"

"Quentin booked her on it. The night before. Said there'd be an important advertiser meeting in Miami. Conveniently, that meeting got canceled. And by then there was the Donna story to deal with."

"Maybe just coincidence," said Jake. "Meetings do get canceled."

"All the time," Claire agreed. "But then there was the powwow in Jacqueline's room. The one that got me so ticked off, where they decided on the spin. I've been thinking back to that meeting. It was Jacqueline who ran with the mistaken identity angle. She ran with it so hard that it seemed like it was her idea. But it wasn't. It was Quentin's. He put it out there very quietly and then backed off, knowing that she'd do the rest. He even gave her credit for the concept. Vintage Quentin. Use people and let them feel good about it."

"Okay, okay," said Jake, "so he's good at pushing buttons, manipulating people. We already know that. That's his job. I still don't see—"

"Why I'm scared stiff?" Claire cut in. Her voice was pinched and her jaw tense in a way Jake had never seen before "I'll tell you why. It's because I think Quentin has lost the line between real life and his precious show. He keeps weaving like a drunk driver between the two, like he can't tell a story line from a real person getting through the day. I'm not sure he sees any difference between a dead character and a dead actress."

"Now wait a second—"

But the limo was turning onto the side road for Big Sandy Key, and Claire didn't wait a second.

"Maybe it's just me," she said. "My nerves are shot. I'm on overload. I admit it. That's why I wanted you along. Do a gut check for me. See what you think. Tell me I'm wrong. Please. Because I just have the feeling that if we don't do something someone's going to die tonight and it won't just be a television death."

48

Beyond the rickety barge landing, things at first seemed fairly normal to Jake, or at least as normal as they ever were around a set. It was night by now but here and there, on a strip of beach or amid a cluster of limp palms, patches of ersatz day had been created by arc lights and reflectors. Thick bundled cables snaked across the ground, imitating mangrove roots; buffered microphones hung from trees like wooly fruit. Cameramen munched their ever-present donuts as they set up angles; make-up people swanned past with their spray bottles and brushes.

After a couple of minutes of wandering, Jake and Claire spotted Quentin Dole at the edge of a clearing, deep in conversation with his director, contemplating a hole in the ground. Four large men were standing hip-deep in the hole, chipping at strata of coral and tangles of ancient roots and stems, flinging shovelsful of debris over their heaving shoulders.

From a few steps away, hidden by the shadows, Jake took a moment to study the producer. He looked tense and drawn and tired; but he'd always looked tense and drawn and tired. His eyes seemed furtive behind the glasses that darkened and lightened as his gaze flicked back and forth in the artificial twilight; but that was as it ever was. In that moment he seemed, as usual, to be locked in a small skirmish of wills he was confident that he would win. Rob Stanton was saying, "Look, I'm not even sure Candace will do this scene. She won't do stunts. It's in her contract."

"This is not a stunt," said Dole. "She steps through a *papier mache* beach into a three-foot hole with padding at the bottom. That's not a stunt."

"Then what is it?" the director asked.

Dodging the question, the producer said, "She'll do it. She has to. It's a great scene and there's no one else." Considering the matter settled, he went back to studying the hole.

Jake and Claire stepped forward toward the light, and when Quentin finally noticed them his face underwent a quick but labored and somehow mechanical change, as though there were gears in his jaw that changed his expression click by click. He managed his usual affable smile and said his usual affable hello. He had the presence of mind to ask Jake how his book was going. Jake lied and said just fine. Dole even asked when he might see some pages.

"Um, pages?" Jake said. "Soon."

It was a clumsy answer but it didn't seem to matter because Dole wasn't really listening. He gave a casual nod in Jake's direction but his eyes and his attention were being ineluctably drawn back to the deepening hole. It was a damp hole with milky gray water oozing in, and in its lower part it gleamed. The shovels rasped and rang as they bit into the hard cake of muck and gravel, setting off tiny landslides that clattered on the workmen's shoes; the wet spoil hit the ground with a satisfying slap as it was tossed away. By millimeters the hole got deeper and everyone just stood there watching it grow.

The four big men chattered softly as they worked, their words muffled by the sounds of digging. But someone must have said something funny because a sudden tide of laughter came up from the hole. One laugh stood out from the others, higher in pitch, more manic in cadence. It was an incongruous high titter of a laugh that sounded like an oboe with a splintered reed.

Jake wheeled and for just a second stared in the direction of the unlikely giggle. The man in the ditch looked up then quickly down. Jake willed him to lift his face but he didn't do it. He stared a heartbeat longer then he blinked at Claire. She shot him a curious look but said nothing. He shuffled his feet and announced abruptly that he needed to get back to town. He was already walking as he said it and Claire had no choice but to follow. Quentin Dole, fascinated by the progress of his artificial sinkhole, said nothing as they left.

They moved quickly and silently across the islet's jarring and unnatural patchwork of light and dark, past tents and sheds and wardrobe racks, and it wasn't until they'd ridden the barge across the channel and were in the limo once again that Jake felt able to bring in a normal breath. Feeling suddenly feverish, he blurted out, "There's something very wrong about that ditch."

Claire said, "But Quentin. How did Quentin seem to you?"

Jake stuck with the hole in the ground. "Those weren't just construction guys. One of them at least works for Charlie Ponte. He was a bodyguard when I went there to find Ace. He pushed me back into my chair. With one hand. It was like a house fell on my shoulders."

"Charlie Ponte? What's Charlie Ponte got to do with it?"

"I have no idea. But it can't be anything good."

The limo rolled across Big Sandy. At the junction with Route 1 the red light caught them and they sat there for a while as drunks weaved past and RVs crawled along. Scratching his head, unconsciously rocking as he thought, Jake said, "The last page of the script."

Claire said, "What about it?"

"The very last page. What happens?"

"Lulu dies. I told you that."

"No," he said. "After. There's got to be a little more. Something. A final beat. How does it actually end?"

She told him.

He nodded so emphatically that hair spilled down across his forehead. "That's it. That's the part we can't let happen."

"Great. And how do we stop it? We call the police and say we have this crazy hunch?"

Jake was sitting far forward on the limo seat, chewing on his knuckles. "We don't stop it."

"But you just said—"

"We don't stop it," Jake repeated. "We let it play out. We just add one small twist. A twist that even Quentin didn't think of."

Claire said, "Jake, I'm just not sure I follow—"

He didn't try to answer that. He'd thrown himself back against the limo seat then squeezed himself into a corner of the car, his fists pressed against his chin. At the edge of Old Town he finally said, "I think I have it. I think I have the pieces. It's a little crazy but it just might work. We're going to need a team."

"A team?"

"A team," said Jake and he started slapping pockets, looking for his phone.

49

By the time Jake and Claire headed back to the set, shortly before midnight, Jake's cottage was strewn with oily pizza boxes and unwashed plates and coffee cups, the detritus left behind by an improbable troupe of allies. Many scraps of paper had been filled with Claire's mysterious diagrams, and Jake's cheap and wrinkled notebook had been splotched with hasty jottings that no one but himself could possibly decipher.

The roads were nearly empty at that hour and the ride back to Big Sandy was a swift one. But after that the long tense night was mostly spent in waiting. Waiting to be ferried across from the now busy barge landing. Waiting for stylists to finish their small touches. Waiting for sound checks, for adjustments to the lighting, for retakes of botched lines. The night grew cool and slightly misty, funky and sensual aromas wafting up from the ground and at the tide line. The uneventful hours dragged by slowly. Quentin Dole lingered at the edges of scenes, saying little, revealing nothing. The fake sinkhole had been artfully covered with a thin crust of phony beach. If Jake and Claire looked very closely they could just barely see the seam where the treacherous cap overlay true earth.

Candace McBride's pick-up was not until four a.m., and by then the diva had gone through many mutations of mood and outlook. Upon learning that she was being dropped from the show, she'd ranted, she'd screamed, she'd cried. She'd gotten half drunk, popped a pill, and slept a while. By the time she woke up her attitude had thoroughly revised itself. Fuck *Adrift!* She'd outgrown it anyway, she didn't need it anymore. It was only her first real gig and it had done for her exactly what she hoped it would. Now she was on her way to better things. A show of her own, perhaps. Tonight she'd do a last star turn for these ungrateful bastards, and after that, the hell with them.

Imagining she was more sober and composed than in fact she was, she put on make-up and got into her clothes. Once installed in the back of her limo, she switched on her reading light and studied her script. Determined that tonight she would actually learn her lines and speak them with no goofs, she paid no attention to the progress of her car as it slipped through town and up the highway.

So she was completely unprepared when the limo came to an abrupt and screeching halt on the lightless road that traversed Big Sandy Key.

Flailing an arm, awkwardly bracing, she was about to start berating her driver when she squinted through the windshield and saw a very old blind man standing on the pavement, just on the crown of the narrow road, not more than ten feet from the car. He stood there motionless and spectral in the ice-blue glare of the high beams, painfully stooped over a white-tipped cane. Pathetically, he was being guided through the blank and hazardous night by a jumpy little chihuahua that strained on its leash and seemed just as lost as he was.

Shaken by the near collision, the limo driver said, "Shit. Where'd that old guy come from? I have to get him off the road."

Candace said, "Oh Christ, honk and go around him. We're late."

But the driver, a kindly sort, got out of the car. He was halfway to his near-victim when Bert wheeled and pulled a gun on him.

It was a small gun, a .25 millimeter that in the old days he'd sometimes worn strapped to his calf. It had not been fired in many years and in fact there were no bullets in it now. Still, it was a gun. Bert told the driver to freeze and the baffled Samaritan thought it prudent to do so.

That was when Bryce clambered up from the mangroves, brandishing an unwieldy but fearsome weapon with blades that clattered and blurred. He strode up to the limousine and with his free hand yanked open the back door. To Candace he said, "You. Out of the car."

The actress didn't budge. In that first moment she was more confused than terrified, an effect of her lingering sedation.

"Come on," Bryce ordered. "Out. Don't make me use the chain saw."

Very slowly, pushing up on hands that were now, belatedly, beginning to tremble, Candace slid across the seat. When she'd gotten closer to the door and had a better look at the man who was threatening her, she said, "Wait a second. That's not a chain saw. It's a hedge trimmer."

The observation put a dent in Bryce's commanding tone. More softly, asking nicely, he said, "Please. Get out of the car. No one's going to hurt you."

She stepped out cautiously and by reflex put her hands up, her position mimicking that of her driver.

Almost apologetically, Bryce said, "You're going to have to take your clothes off."

"Oh my God," said Candace.

"Over here," said Bryce. Gesturing with the hedge trimmer he directed her toward the steeply sloping shoulder of the road where an ancient El Dorado convertible was hidden by the mangroves. Unsteady on her quaking knees, the actress lightly leaned against the car. "Now take 'em off," Bryce said.

"Oh my God," she said again.

Gallantly, he said, "I won't watch."

"You won't?"

Bryce turned away and Candace stripped. She wasn't wearing much and it didn't take long. She stepped out of her sandals, let her shorts slip down around her ankles, undid the buttons of her low-cut blouse and slithered out of it. In the damp night goose bumps appeared at once on her arms and legs and breasts.

A door clicked open on the El Dorado and the interior light came on. Donna Alvarez was sitting in the car, wearing a bathrobe and a jet-black wig and violet-colored contact lenses. The contours of her mouth had been broadened and bowed by a generous application of moistly glistening lipstick; her eyes appeared deeper in their pools of faint lavender shadow; a more dramatic arc had been penciled into her brows.

She swiveled out of the car and said good evening. The naked Candace briefly stared at her, recoiled, then stared some more, perplexed yet compelled by the other woman's rude and shocking imitation of herself.

"You?" she said at last. "Why the hell are you here? What the fuck is going on?"

Donna didn't answer right away. She was staring back at the other woman without prejudice and with unmasked curiosity, the way that only women look at women. She said, "You look beautiful, Candace. You really do."

"Screw you, sister. Now what the—"

"I'm doing you a big fat favor," Donna said. "You'll thank me sometime. Or, knowing you, maybe not. Give me the clothes."

Candace didn't move.

"Do we have to make this unpleasant? I can't bend so well. So reach the fuck down and hand me the clothes."

Never taking her acid stare off Donna, the diva gathered the few garments. Donna slipped out of the robe, wincing just slightly as she freed her right arm, and handed it to her.

From up on the pavement, Bert called out, "What about the driver's clothes. We need his too? I can't remember."

"Just the cap," said Bryce. "I think the cap is a nice touch."

50

Sunrise waits for no one, and the carjacking had used up precious minutes of remaining night. By the time the jauntily hatted Bryce delivered Donna to the landing, opening the door for her and offering his hand as she requested, the gauzy stars were dimming and the whole world seemed wrapped up in a last delicious dream before another day began.

She rode the barge across the channel. On the other side, emerging from the weird checkerboard of humid darkness and harsh fake light, Jake and Claire were there to meet her. Behind them, bleary-eyed crew were lugging gear; exhausted cast members sat on stumps or leaned limply against trees.

"Everything go smoothly?" Jake asked in a whisper.

"Well, I'm here," said Donna. "And the filming?"

"Smoothly enough," Claire said. "Just enough behind schedule to make Quentin a nervous wreck. Snapping at people. Biting his nails. Cursing about Candace always being late. All good stuff. You ready?"

Donna nodded firmly. She was always ready. "I look okay?"

"You look beautiful," said Jake. "Leading lady beautiful. Walk between us. Stay close."

Keeping to the fringes of the light, stepping over cables, dodging tents and sheds, swatting spider webs, they made their way across the islet to the clearing where the big scene was to be shot. A campfire was burning there, its yellow pyramid of flame stretching and receding, blurring and smearing whatever was behind it. Shadowy people milled and paced. From twenty feet away came the faint hiss of calm water perking through a stony beach.

Quentin Dole and Rob Stanton, their glances flicking back and forth between their watches and the eastern sky, finally saw the diva approaching on the far side of the clearing. The director called out, "Hello, Candace. Glad you could make it."

Donna swallowed, summoned focus, then tried out her Candace voice, breathy and sardonic, a voice she'd studied for months and rehearsed in the bathtub a hundred times. "Stupid time to shoot a scene," she said. "Be goddamn glad I'm here at all."

The director let it pass, as he had let so many comments pass. Instead he shouted, "Make-up. Is make-up ready?"

There was an instant of secret panic before Claire answered, "She's all made up. She's good to go."

"All right then," Stanton said. "Let's get this done. And let's please get it right the first time, okay? Positions. Lights."

Donna stepped out from the shadows and took up an aloof and haughty stance near the fire, arms crossed against her midriff, face turned stubbornly away.

Her fellow actor, playing Lulu's latest suitor, struck a pleading pose, leaning forward, arms outstretched.

Soft dim lights came up through scrims. The light was bluish lavender, a distillation of the color of the night itself.

The director called for action and the suitor, swaying and pacing in what was almost a dance, launched into his speech. He'd been mad for Lulu from the moment he'd seen her. Hadn't she even noticed the way he looked at her? The way he plotted to be near her, to steal a little time alone?...

The speech went on but Jake and Claire weren't listening. They were watching Quentin Dole. He was standing at the clearing's edge, the restless campfire reflected in his glasses. His fists were balled, his shoulders hunched. At moments he seemed to be mouthing the dialogue he'd written. Now and then his gaze was tugged toward the place where the hole in the ground was covered by its flimsy sheath of sand and paper and plaster.

The suitor continued his wooing. He could make Lulu happy, he knew he could. So what if they were far away from everything they'd known before? Wasn't that what lovers really wanted? To be alone, without distractions, without history. To invent their own idea of paradise...

He left off on that beckoning note and the cameras pivoted toward Donna. She paused before she spoke; it was a brief but resonant interval in which her face revealed nuances that her character had never shown before. The toughness tempered by hurt; the hard shell imperfectly hiding the disappointed heart of a romantic child. In her voice, a veneer of bitterness gave way to a soft core of something sorrowful and tender.

LULU

Paradise...I guess this place could seem like Paradise. For some
people. Maybe for you. Not for me. I see it clearly now: for
me this place is hell. It's hell because I don't feel anything. I
don't feel hope. I don't feel fear. Most of all, I don't feel love.
(a pause)
You know, it's funny. Well, almost funny. People talk about the
pain of unrequited love. Like loving someone who doesn't love
you back is the worst thing that can happen. It isn't. Because loving gives you something, something wonderful, even if you aren't
loved in return. No, my pain is worse. Not being able to love at
all. Being chosen but never choosing. Being desired and never
feeling desire in return. You can't know what that emptiness is
like...No, there's nothing for me here. Absolutely nothing.

It seemed that no one breathed during the speech. The trees didn't stir; the wavelets didn't break. It took a heartbeat's worth of silence to jump-start life again. Then fronds rustled softly and foam fizzed over rocks. The red rim of the sun lifted from the ocean, seeming to shake off water as it rose. With a last look back, a look that said goodbye not only to her would-be lover but to all the things she knew would never be, Lulu began to walk away.

She took one step, two steps. On the third step her foot found the plaster cap of beach and she crashed abruptly through it. Her posture never changed as she vanished. She plummeted downward as streamlined as a diver. She didn't scream, didn't whimper. She simply disappeared without complaint, as if she was grateful that the earth had swallowed her.

"Cut!" yelled Rob Stanton. Then, toward the vacant place where Lulu had last been standing, he called out, "My God, Candace, that was brilliant, stunning, perfect. Where you been keeping that intensity?"

No answer came forth from the hole in the ground. The sun kept rising, almost the whole red disk now lifted from the sea. Arc lights were switched off, cameras shifted.

The director shouted, "Come on out now, Candace. One last scene to shoot."

There was no sound or movement from the hole.

Half a minute went by. Jake and Claire were watching Quentin Dole. Veins stood out in his neck and twin blood-red suns were rising in his glasses. He couldn't seem to keep his feet quite still.

Rob Stanton called out for Candace once again, and when she didn't answer he said, "Come on, no time for games."

He started walking toward the hole. Quentin matched him stride for stride, Jake and Claire half a step behind.

But before anybody reached the ravaged plaster cap there was an apparition.

Donna was rising up through it. She wasn't climbing; she was ascending. She rose vertically and very slowly, as arrow-straight as how she'd entered, her face serene, eyes calm, neck and shoulders only gradually emerging. Dole saw her rising and froze where he stood.

Jake, close at his side now, said, "Surprised, Quentin?"

The producer said nothing, just flicked his eyes this way and that.

"She wasn't supposed to come out of there, was she, Quentin?"

Stammering, he said, "I have no idea what you're talking about."

"Yes you do," Claire put in. She was standing at the producer's other flank, shaking a script as she spoke. "It's right here. You wrote it yourself."

"That?" he said dismissively. "That's just television." He gestured spasmodically toward Donna, whose torso was now above the level of the ground. "But this...this is..."

"This is what?" Jake said. "This is—or was supposed to be—your ultimate coup, the buzz to end all buzzes. A real death on your show. The star, no less. Who'd gotten to be a problem for you anyway. Perfect."

Dole shook his head. He even managed a faint laugh. As was his custom when trapped, he didn't argue, just tried a different tactic. "You're a storyteller, Jake. You're making up your own plot here."

"No, it's not my story. It's yours. Especially that final scene. The one where they find Lulu at the bottom of a six-foot sinkhole, pierced through by an old buried stump that had been ground down sharp as a spear."

"Television," the producer said. "The magic of television. We break the scene, do a mock-up of the wound, some phony blood..."

"When did the hole get six feet deep?" Claire asked. "It was three when we were here."

The question briefly flummoxed Dole. Then he said, "Three, six, what's the difference? It's only—"

He broke off abruptly because just then the rest of Donna rose up from the hole. Her feet, in muddy sandals, were firmly propped on two enormous hands. She stepped from them onto solid ground. Then a giant fist punched through the wafer of beach, and behind it came Ace's head and shoulders. Almost casually the big man said, "And here's your murder weapon."

He tossed a shaft of casuarina, also known as ironwood for its freakish hardness, out of the hole and onto the beach, where it rolled a few inches then stopped. It was the thickness of a closet pole, maybe four feet long, and had been whittled to a vicious point.

Ace braced his hands on the edge of the hole and lifted out easily, like a swimmer from a pool, before continuing. "Was stuck in the bottom, sticking straight up. Almost got me when I climbed down. Had to work like crazy to wrestle it out. Woulda killed someone for sure."

The sun had risen higher and was spilling orange light across the scene. The damp hole glistened. The pointed shaft of ironwood softly gleamed. For a moment no one spoke and the only sound was a very faint mechanical whine, perhaps the distant chatter of an engine.

Claire said, "You were going to film it, weren't you, Quentin? Bring a camera over, find the body. Make television history. The final merger of real life and your show."

Dole was shaking his head, in fact his whole body, in denial. "This is nonsense, craziness. I don't know anything about some pointy stick. Look, nothing happened. No one got hurt. Why don't we just forget—"

He didn't finish the sentence because quite suddenly the faint mechanical whine had deepened into a guttural roar as a speedboat rounded a turn and rocketed toward the beach. Up on plane, the wake humping outward like a miniature tsunami, the craft split the water, vermilion spray flying from its hull. For a moment it appeared that the hurtling boat would run up onto land, but then the engines were abruptly cut and it subsided quickly, rocking as it settled. The sun was on its stern. In its cockpit a single figure was silhouetted, its exact contours blotted out by glare.

The figure raised an arm. Dull blue metal glinted and in that instant Jake knew, more quickly than by reason, who the figure was and where the gun was aimed. He didn't speak, didn't shout, had no thought of risk or courage, just threw himself at Donna's legs as the bullet meant for Candace left the muzzle. They rolled together on the knobby beach and the shot found Quentin Dole instead. It hit him in the chest. For a moment he stood very still, the image of a tall blonde woman reflected in his glasses, a puzzled look twisting his thin lips, as though he was trying to rethink a scene gone wrong. Then his legs gave way and he fell, his arms stretched toward the hole in the ground, his weakly twitching hands grasping at the shoveled earth.

51

"The way I see it," Joey Goldman was saying, "his story was gonna be that the hole got deeper by itself. Ya know, caved in, the way real sinkholes happen or empty swimming pools cave in. Pressure down there. Happens. So it caves in and exposes the old tree trunk and there's a horrible accident in front of plenty of witnesses. Hard to prove, hard to disprove."

"Except," said Ace, "we caught guys digging. Around eleven, when everyone had left. We watched from Joey's boat. They took the fake beach off, dug some more, planted the spike, put the top back on. Then they got in this dinghy that was stashed in the mangroves and rowed away. Joey put me ashore and I hid down in the hole. Disgusting down there, lemme tell ya. Plus I almost took the spear right up my ass. Who wants more grouper? I got like a whole other batch here."

It was evening and everyone had gathered at the compound. Placid blue light gleamed above the pool. Seagulls soared above the streetlights and palm fronds rattled softly in the breeze. The mood was almost festive but not quite, tempered by fatigue and a grudging but undeniable sympathy for the death of Quentin Dole; and for the incarcerated future of the tall and crazy blonde, who'd been arrested, without resistance and apparently with relief, the instant she stepped ashore at the Brigantine Marina; for the flash-in-the-pan hit show called *Adrift,* on which work was now suspended and which was nearly certain to be canceled; and even for Candace McBride, who'd been upstaged in her own death scene and was already headed back to California without a show, without a role, the media furious at her, her meteoric career suddenly a cinder. So the gathering wasn't boisterous, wasn't gloating, and yet it was celebratory, a happy but muted ceremony by a very tired winning team.

Holding out his plate for more fish, Jake said, "The part I couldn't figure was why Charlie Ponte was involved. When I saw that bodyguard working in the ditch, the one with the crazy laugh—"

"Tiny," Ace put in. "His name is Tiny. I saw him this afternoon when I delivered the blonde's boat to Ponte. Grabbed it before the cops did. Used it to repay a favor and say goodbye forever. Anyway, so Tiny tells me what I already figured, that it wasn't Ponte that hired those guys to dig the hole. It was Handsome Johnny. He borrowed a crew, just like he borrowed me to steal the script."

"But why?" Claire asked. "Why would Handsome Johnny be involved at all?"

The question hung for a moment and no one realized what a melancholy question it was. Handsome Johnny had been involved because he very briefly knew a son for whom he would do anything, and who now, abruptly, had vanished from his life as though he'd never been fathered.

Gesturing with his wineglass, Bert the Shirt offered a different theory. "Handsome Johnny was involved because he's a worthless little pissant who likes to pretend he's in show business." He drank some wine then said, almost as an afterthought, "Wonder who he hired to run y'over."

Donna said, "Excuse me?"

"Wasn't Ace," Bert said.

"Wouldn't'a been the blonde," the big man put in, "since she had a script and woulda known it wasn't Candace in the water."

"Right," said Bert, "and now we find out Johnny was in cahoots with the producer guy. Bingo. Wonder who he hired to do the dirty work."

Claire said, "You don't think he drove the boat himself?"

"Handsome Johnny Burke?" Bert said dismissively. "Take on a risk like that? Take a chance on being the fall guy? Not for love or money."

In this he underestimated the small-time mobster who'd fled from Hollywood only to make a second mess in Florida.

The platter of fish was passed around. More wine was poured. Donna ate and drank left-handed; her sling was back in place. Claire asked her how her arm was.

"Hurts like a bastard. But it's worth it. I finally had a speaking part."

Claire said, "And your performance was dazzling, amazing."

The former stuntwoman gave a modest and lopsided shrug.

"How'd you do it?" Claire went on. "How'd you just step in like that and get so deep in Lulu's character, the sadness, the hopelessness?"

Donna nibbled some grouper before she answered. "Little secret? In my mind I wasn't playing Lulu. I was playing Candace. I was thinking: what's going on inside this person, or isn't, to make her such a bitch? That's where it all came from."

"Well, it worked," Jake said.

A little cocky now, Donna said, "Hey, I told you I could do it, right? The very first night we talked. I said I could nail that fucking role if I ever got the chance. I just thought I never would. And I wouldn't have if Bryce and Bert didn't pull off the hijacking so well."

Bryce beamed. "I loved that part. That part was really fun. The hedge clippers—"

"Hedge-clippers," Ace put in. "Dustbuster. What next, a fucking Vegematic?"

Bryce said, "I'll improvise, I'll see what comes to hand. Maybe a gun with no bullets, like Bert."

The old man shook his head and his huge nose lightly fanned the table. "I'll tell ya, bullets, no bullets, it felt really lousy to have a gun in my hand again. But what can I say? Ya gotta do what ya gotta do. I'll tell ya, though, I felt bad for the driver. Nice guy, this is what he gets. What a fucking world…But the blind man shtick, this is what I'm proud of. Pulled that off good. Couldn't've done it without Nacho here. The guide dog. Played his part great. Didn't ya, Nacho?"

He scratched the chihuahua under the chin and its drooping whiskers tickled his knuckles.

A moment later Joey said, "Nacho. You called him Nacho."

"What of it? That's his name, ain't it?"

"Yeah, but—"

"I know, I know. I used to call him by the other name before. Ya think I didn't know that? But ya gotta understand. When you've had something in your life for a long time, a person, a place, a dog, and then it isn't there no more, it takes a while to get used to it, to admit that something changed. I wasn't ready to let go before. Now I am. I'm ready to let go. Salud."

EPILOGUE

L ate next morning, when the call came in, Jake and Claire were still in bed. Her head was nestled in the crook of his arm, her hair brushed lightly against his cheek. They'd known each other barely a week, but as Claire had once told Jake, television sped up everything, and when they'd made love it had been with an ease and candor usually reserved for longtime partners, for people already shaped to one another in their bodies and their hearts. Being in each other's arms had felt like sailing someplace never seen but also like sailing home again.

But now Jake's phone was ringing, and after some seconds Claire, accustomed to being responsible, accountable, said, "Aren't you going to pick it up?"

"Nah."

"See who it is, at least?"

Jake looked at the screen. "It's my agent."

"In my world," Claire said, "clients take their agent's calls, if not always vice versa."

So Jake shrugged and took the call.

Lou Mermelstein launched right in, as was his custom. "Christ, Jake," he said, "you landed in a real shitstorm down there. The killing, the suspension of the show, it's all over the news. You must be a wreck."

Claire was toying with the whorls of hair along his sternum. He felt the warmth of her leg on top of his. He said, "Actually, I'm okay, I'm fine."

As if he hadn't really heard the answer, the agent went on. "It's a disaster. I mean, there's obviously no tie-in book if there's no show to tie into. But, listen, it shouldn't be a total loss, I just spoke to the publisher. Given the crazy circumstances, they're willing to pay a kill fee. They offered twenty-five. I'm pushing for fifty. I said you've been breaking your ass on this book, it's like half drafted already. Whaddya think?"

Jake said, "I don't want a kill fee."

Mermelstein said, "You don't seem to understand. If there's no—"

"I haven't written a word of the stupid tie-in book and I don't want a penny for it."

Rather sternly the agent said, "Jake, I have a reputation to protect. I can't say no to money."

"Who's saying no? I'm saying I want the whole two hundred grand. But I want it for a different book. I want to write about what really happened."

"What really happened?" echoed Mermelstein. "What happened is that some deranged fan took a pot shot at the creator of the show. End of story. Tabloid stuff. I don't see a book there."

"Except that's not what happened. Not even close."

"No? Okay, so you tell me. What really happened? Let's hear the pitch."

Jake wriggled higher on his pillows, Claire slinking alongside. Trusting to the moment, he improvised a spiel about three speedboats, some Mafia, an impossible diva, a tirelessly profane stuntwoman, an old man with a dog, a suicidal brother, a tough guy with a heart of gold, a slacker with a Dustbuster, a television genius going off the rails, a compound offering peace and mayhem, and an on-location romance between a line producer and a ghostwriter.

The agent said, "Jesus Christ. Is that what really happened?"

"Pretty much," said Jake.

"Sit tight," the agent said. "I'll call the publisher and get back to you."

Jake's book was called *The Stuntwoman and the Diva* and it caught on in a way his earlier real-name efforts never had. Within days of its release it went viral among the many fans of *Adrift* who were still in mourning for the loss of their favorite show. From that core group of impassioned and in-the-know readers, the audience broadened and the momentum built, until the book became one of those must-read items on the grab-and-go tables of every airport and on the welcome page of every electronic bookstore. A hefty film deal quickly followed.

Jake and Claire were bicoastal in those giddy months, she, as lead producer, based in L.A. to deal with the studio and the actors' agents; he, as screenwriter, flying in for meetings with the suits then returning to the haven of the compound to soak up local atmosphere and revisit the beaches and bars and islets where the story was set. But once the script had been approved and the shooting was scheduled to begin, the lovers were together nearly every night, either in Jake's yellow cottage or at Claire's quite grand suite at The Nest.

The movie was released the following winter, and at Claire's insistence the world premiere was held not in New York or Los Angeles but in Key West, in a small theater on a narrow street in a miniature town where people sometimes surprised themselves and changed their lives. Reviews were generally excellent, rhapsodizing especially about the debut performance of Donna Alvarez, who appeared seemingly from nowhere to brilliantly carry off the dual roles of the stand-in and the star.

In preparation for the post-premiere party, the red carpet had been unfurled in front of Ace's Place, a recent arrival on the downtown scene and by all accounts the place to go for seafood. Cameras rolled as the notables stepped out of their limousines and filed in. Inside, champagne flowed, toasts were proposed, cheeks were kissed and backs were patted. In the weeks that followed the nationwide opening, the usual Oscar buzz and rumors gathered steam. But *Stuntwoman* wasn't destined for an Oscar. It just wasn't that kind of movie. It didn't push the envelope or proclaim its own importance. It was neither more nor less than a small, peculiar story that had a few good lines and some characters who might be fun to have a drink with, and that turned out as it should.

Books by Laurence Shames

Key West Mysteries:
Florida Straits
Scavenger Reef
Sunburn
Tropical Depression
Virgin Heat
Mangrove Squeeze
Welcome to Paradise
The Naked Detective

Other Books by Laurence Shames
The Big Time: The Harvard Business School's Most Successful Class
    & How It Shaped America
The Hunger for More: Searching for Values in an Age of Greed
The Angels' Share—A Novel of Life After California

Collaborations:
Boss of Bosses: The Fall of the Godfather: The FBI and Paul
    Castellano, by Joseph F. O'Brien & Andris Kurins
Not Fade Away: A Short Life Well Lived, by Laurence Shames and
    Peter Barton
Life is What You Make It: Find Your Own Path to Fulfillment, by
    Peter Buffett
The One World Schoolhouse, by Salman Khan

About the Author

Laurence Shames has been a New York City taxi driver, lounge singer, furniture mover, lifeguard, dishwasher, gym teacher, and shoe salesman. Having failed to distinguish himself in any of those professions, he turned to writing full-time in 1976 and has not done an honest day's work since.

His basic laziness notwithstanding, Shames has published more than twenty books and hundreds of magazine articles and essays. Best known for his critically acclaimed series of Key West novels, he has also authored non-fiction and enjoyed considerable though largely secret success as a collaborator and ghostwriter. Shames has penned four New York Times bestsellers. These have appeared on four different lists, under four different names, none of them his own. This might be a record.

Born in Newark, New Jersey in 1951, to chain-smoking parents of modest means but flamboyant emotions, Shames did not know Philip Roth, Paul Simon, Queen Latifa, Shaquille O'Neal, or any of the other really cool people who have come from his hometown. He graduated summa cum laude from NYU in 1972 and was inducted into Phi Beta Kappa. As a side note, both his alma mater and honorary society have been extraordinarily adept at tracking his many address changes through the decades, in spite of the fact that he's never sent them one red cent.

It was on an Italian beach in the summer of 1970 that Shames first heard the sacred call of the writer's vocation. Lonely and poor, hungry and thirsty, he'd wandered into a seaside trattoria, where he noticed a couple tucking into a big platter of *fritto misto*. The man was nothing much to look at but the woman was really beautiful. She was perfectly tan and had a very fine-gauge gold chain looped around her bare tummy. The couple was sharing a liter of white wine; condensation beaded the carafe. Eye contact was made; the couple turned out to be Americans. The man wiped olive oil from his rather sensual lips and introduced himself as a writer. Shames knew in that moment that he would be one too.

He began writing stories and longer things he thought of as novels. He couldn't sell them.

By 1979 he'd somehow become a journalist and was soon publishing in top-shelf magazines like Playboy, Outside, Saturday Review, and Vanity Fair. (This transition entailed some lucky breaks, but is not as vivid a tale as the *fritto misto* bit, so we'll just sort of gloss over it.) In 1982, Shames was named Ethics columnist of Esquire, and was also made a contributing editor to that magazine.

By 1986 he was writing non-fiction books whose critical, if not commercial, success first established Shames' credentials as a collaborator/ghostwriter. His 1991 national bestseller, Boss of Bosses, written with two FBI agents, got him thinking about the Mafia. It also bought him a ticket out of New York and a sweet little house in Key West, where he finally got back to Plan A: writing novels.

Given his then-current preoccupations, the novels, beginning with the cult classic, Florida Straits, naturally featured palm trees, high humidity, dogs in sunglasses, and New York mobsters blundering through a town where people were too laid back to be afraid of them. Having found a setting he loved and a loyal readership as well, Shames wrote eight Key West novels during the 1990s, six of which were optioned for feature film.

After a twelve-year detour into writing screenplays and non-fiction, Shames has now made a happy and rollicking return to the Keys with *Shot on Location*.

Find him online at http://www.laurenceshames.com

28972464R00121

Made in the USA
Lexington, KY
08 January 2014